CONTESTED VALLEY

Center Point
Large Print

Also by Hunter Ingram and available from
Center Point Large Print:

Fort Apache
Man Hunt
The Long Search

CONTESTED VALLEY

HUNTER INGRAM

CENTER POINT LARGE PRINT
THORNDIKE, MAINE

This Center Point Large Print edition
is published in the year 2025 by arrangement with
Golden West Inc.

Copyright © 1968 by Hunter Ingram.

All rights reserved.

The text of this Large Print edition is unabridged.
In other aspects, this book may vary
from the original edition.
Printed in the United States of America
on permanent paper sourced using
environmentally responsible foresting methods.
Set in 16-point Times New Roman type.

ISBN: 979-8-89164-549-3

The Library of Congress has cataloged this record
under Library of Congress Control Number: 2025930457

CONTESTED VALLEY

Chapter One

The emigrant train was hot, crowded, and dirty, and the passengers' faces were stamped with the varied degrees of their personal discomfort. The long string of cars creaked and groaned as the engine picked up speed on its plunge from the summit. The floor of the California desert rushed to meet the train, and each foot of drop renewed the heat. Most of the four days and nights from Omaha to here had been spent in heat: the summer heat of the seared prairies, the blistering reflection of the sun's rays across Utah's salt-encrusted, barren land, the equal aridness of Nevada's high plains with their persistent, irritating alkali dust. It didn't take much of the wind's stirring to keep great clouds of dust in the air, clouds that enveloped a man until his skin itched with it. Only in the mountains had there been relief—all too short, for the crossing of the cool crest had been brief.

The floors of the cars were huge sounding boards, transmitting each jar and jolt of the rough, uneven roadbed to the passengers with an intensity that turned the flesh numb under the constant hammering. Somewhere up ahead a child cried fretfully, and a mother answered it in cross tones, her own misery too great to hold sympathy at the moment for the child.

The cars were little more than long, narrow boxes on wheels, furnished with unupholstered traverse benches, a wood stove at one end, and a water closet at the other. A row of feeble lamps, suspended from the ceiling, furnished inadequate lighting at night. The sleeping accommodations were sparse; a board cut to fit the space between the facing benches and cotton bags leanly stuffed with straw. Each passenger was expected to furnish his own blankets, or he slept without.

Usually one car was allotted to a family, but that didn't mean the family had ample room. For the car was crammed with household furniture, farm implements, horses, cows, dogs, and cats. Young fruit trees and seed for the first season's planting were jammed into every available nook and cranny. Added to the reek of unwashed human bodies was the overpowering smell of hot animal flesh and the rich, ripe aroma of manure.

Three families shared this car, but they were fortunate, for there was no livestock in it. Oakes Paulson sat solidly on one of the wooden benches, staring in gloomy meditation at the knuckles of his hands. The scenery no longer held interest for him. He was surfeited with scenery. He was hungry, and his rear was a solid mass of intolerable aching. He had tried lifting first one cheek then the other from the hard wooden bench, but that brought no real relief, and the strain of riding in that position was as bad as the pounding. He wondered how the women endured this trip, with their tenderer flesh. Perhaps the padding was deeper and better placed. He smiled with sour humor and let the thought go.

His eyes traced the scar that ran from the knuckle on the first finger of his left hand to his wrist. It was a bad scar, and he remembered the day of its making. He had forced the saw, making it jump its course, and it had laid open his hand. Impatience was his great trouble, and he constantly fought to curb it. But waiting was hard for him, and a job that took painstaking care was infinitely galling. Those broad, blunt fingers and huge hands would never be the master of delicate, fine work.

He closed his hands, and the knuckles stood out like small, jutting rocks. But those hands could be gentle with sick livestock, or a plant that needed additional care.

The hands fitted the body. His size caught men's attention and put respect in them. His shoulders were massive, his chest deep. He moved on legs as sturdy as tree trunks. The family legend said he was named for those legs. His father had looked at the new baby with pride. "Look at those legs. They're like small oak trees."

Oakes Paulson had an oak tree's practical appearance. There was nothing gentle or graceful about him. And he had the oak's characteristics. He stood planted firmly, and he shattered opposition, or it shattered him. His hair was a tousled dark brown mop, almost black in certain light. His face was hewn with rough strokes, at first glance harsh-appearing and forbidding. His forehead was wide, the chin square and jutting. The deep-set eyes could glow like a fire in a cave when they were sparked by the too-ready temper. But there was a softness in them, too, a sad quality, and the lips could be mobile in laughter. Women's eyes lingered on his face, sensing a strength, a protectiveness in it, and men, recognizing its force, viewed it with speculative eyes and put their challenges elsewhere.

"Damn," he grunted, as the car hit a particularly rough spot. The ensuing jolt slammed the bench against his already sensitive butt.

He let his eyes rove about the car. The Wallaces occupied the front part of it. Ben Wallace was a shriveled little man in his forties, the juices of life already drying in him. Myra, his wife, was a sad-faced, gaunt woman with a whining petulance at life's harshness.

The Andersons occupied the rear end of the car. They were fat, with fat people's joviality, and not too clean. A man kept a high wall erected between himself and the Andersons, or they spilled over and absorbed him.

It hit Oakes with sudden force that this train was made up of people of the same ilk: the shiftless, the hard-luck ones, the beaten people.

All of them running from one piece of land to another, blaming their misfortune on the land they had just left and with only the prospect of finding more of the same ahead. It angered Oakes to think he was among this breed. There had been no need to leave Ohio land. It had responded to the exact degree that a man gave to it. California land would be the same. Why throw up everything seeking what one already had? He had two answers to that: one a promise he had made to his dying mother. "You're stronger than Ross, Oakes. Look after him." It was an odd role, a younger brother looking after an older one, but no new load. He had shouldered it for as long as he could remember. All through their growing-up years, he had fought Ross's fights and done most of his work. Oakes had his mother's strength and determination, Ross took after his father. His mother had seen that, and her deepest concern had always been placed in the weaker one. That was one reason. The other was Josie, Ross's wife.

Oakes let his eyes rest on her in a long, thorough evaluation, knowing he would find what he always found. Some things were made to endure, and his feeling for her was one of them. He couldn't help coveting her in his thoughts, but he prided himself that no one else knew. He could look at her and begin nibbling on his heart again, and it was sad, solitary fare.

She sat across the aisle from him, her head

turned as she gazed at something out of the window. His eyes traced the clean line of her jaw. She was twenty-three, two years younger than himself, and there was a tough quality about her, for physical work and blows at the spirit couldn't scar or dent her too badly. His anger always rose when he thought of Ross's restless eye, and he wondered if she knew. The old saying was that a wife was always the last to know. He thought it more probable she was the last to admit it.

She was graceful when she was still and graceful when she moved, and whatever a man needed should have been found in her. Her eyes and lips were made for laughter, though he seldom saw it anymore. And that always increased his nameless anger.

His scrutiny touched her, and she turned her head and smiled at him. She had deep blue eyes with a fathomless mystery that should have taken a man a lifetime to explore. He thought of the shallow eyes that caught Ross's interest, and his eyes smoldered.

He stood and moved to her, balancing his body against the lurching of the car. She moved her skirts, and he sat down beside her. "Josie, how do you manage to always stay so fresh?"

She made a small grimace. "I'm not. It's the perfume you smell. Women have that advantage over men."

"Then I should borrow that advantage. And you

should tell Bess Anderson about it." Standing next to Bess Anderson was overpowering.

Josie darted a quick glance to the rear of the car to be sure she wasn't overheard, then laughed. "Poor Bess. She tries so hard. Don't be too harsh on her, Oakes."

He stared soberly at her. She forgave a weakness easily, and he always felt chastened at the measuring of his own nature against hers.

The engine went into a sweeping curve. It changed the wind direction blowing through the car. He sniffed at it and said, "Damn."

"What is it, Oakes?"

"I thought I smelled it earlier this morning. Anderson's got tongue in this car again."

She touched his arm as he stood. "Easy, Oakes."

He frowned at her before he moved to the rear of the car. No man's forgiveness should be expected to be big enough to include spoiled tongue. Tongue was either cheap, or it was Anderson's favorite food, for this had happened in Nebraska and again in Nevada. Tongue turned bad in a few hours of heat, and its stink was unbearable.

Anderson stared out the window, and Oakes's touch on his shoulder turned him.

Oakes saw the food box under the bench. "Have you got tongue in there again?"

"I told him to throw it out last night." Bess Anderson's lips parted in a foolish smile. She was a fawning woman, trying desperately for attention.

Oakes didn't look at her as he stooped to pick up the box.

Anderson grabbed Oakes's wrist as he straightened. "Here now. You're making pretty free with another man's property."

His truculence faded under Oakes's eyes, and his hand fell away. "I guess I forgot it."

Oakes pitched the box out of the window. "If you want your tongue, eat it. Don't try to store it up."

Anderson couldn't meet his eyes. "All right. All right."

As Oakes turned away he heard the man say to his wife, "You'd better learn to keep your fat mouth shut." He walked back to Josie and sat down.

Her eyes reproved him. "Are you satisfied? They're quarreling."

"Is that my fault? If he had something to say, why didn't he say it to me?"

"You know why, Oakes. He was there, too, when the engine went off the track. He saw you help pry it back on."

Oakes scowled. A lot of the passengers gave him most of the credit for that, and he had seen the glistening regard of women as they looked at his arms. "Damn it, Josie. There were twenty of us prying at that engine." The seventeen-ton engine had jumped the track in Nebraska. The derailment wasn't bad enough to warrant calling out the wrecker. A nearby fence had been stripped of posts, and the engine levered back onto the track. Oakes wanted his part in the incident forgotten, but apparently it stayed fresh in people's minds.

She shook her head. "You're quarrelsome, Oakes. You have been ever since we left Ohio."

He stared with fixed concentration at the knuckles of his hand. "Why shouldn't I be? Are you happy with this move?"

"I go where Ross goes."

He probed her eyes and saw no lie in them. Even if she was unhappy, she would never be disloyal enough to Ross to admit it.

"Just because Ross decided on this, it makes it all right?"

"You didn't have to come." Her words were accompanied by the quick, hot flare in her eyes.

He attempted a grin, and it came off not too badly. "I don't want to fight with you, Josie."

She was easily mollified, and she touched his arm and smiled. "It's been a hard trip on all of us."

That flicked him in a sensitive place. "You think it's the hardships I'm complaining about?"

She shook her head. She had never heard him complain about a physical hardship.

"I can take riding in this cattle car, Josie.

But little things keep happening that make me wonder how far we can trust this railroad. We've had to bribe the train crew to stop at stations where we can get something to eat. If we don't pay, they stop where there's no food. There's crooked gamblers on the train and peddlers of fake jewelry. Yes, and thieves. I heard Jenkins trying to tell the conductor his money was stolen last night. The conductor just shrugged him off."

Her face was troubled. "Unity told me about it this morning. I'm sorry for them. But anyone could have taken it. I don't see how the railroad can be blamed."

"It's the railroad's responsibility to protect its passengers. Even the kind of passengers we are. Did they warn us against thieves and gamblers? They did not. I do blame them."

He pulled a well-creased circular from his pocket. The railroad had blanketed the eastern part of the country with these circulars inviting settlers onto railroad land. The circulars were effective, pulling long trainloads of people to California. He didn't have to look at the paper, for he knew its wording by heart.

"Do you believe what they say here, Josie?"

Worry lay deep in her eyes. "We've got to believe them. We're not out anything yet, are we? We've given them no money."

Ross had said practically the same thing. "We're not? We're out the cost of the trip. We're thinking of settling on land before patents are issued. They promise us that's all we'll need, that just the settling gives us preference over later applicants. They promise not to take any improvements into consideration when they finally fix the price." He slapped the circular with a violence that tore it. "There's nothing definite here, Josie. Some vague promises and too many 'ifs.' I want to walk up, pay my money, and get my patent."

His vehemence sparked a response in her. "You didn't have to sell because we did. You didn't have to come."

He frowned at her. "We owned the land together. I had to agree to sell for Ross to get his money." He made a helpless gesture. "As long as I had to buy new land, I might as well buy it in California as in Ohio." That wasn't the major reason for his decision at all. He would be lost without Ross and even more so without Josie.

Some hostility was between them, a vague blaming of each other for their present predicament. "Don't worry about me, Josie. I'll do what I think I have to."

"Including fighting the railroad?"

He wanted to see the disapproving look gone from her face, and he said with wry humor, "I promise not to fight the railroad without cause." Her eyes didn't light as much as he wanted, and he wondered if Ross was the cause. "Where's Ross?"

She wouldn't look at him. "I haven't seen him for the past several hours."

He had the impulse to reach out and cover her hand. She wasn't entirely blind. That little Mrs. Lowden, with the bold eyes, had made too many trips through this car. When Oakes found Mrs. Lowden, he would find Ross.

"I'll hunt him up. You kept the sale money, didn't you, Josie?"

He swore at the guilt in her eyes, and her temper flashed. "The money belongs to him as much as to you and I. Quit treating him like a baby."

"I will when he quits behaving like one." He stalked toward the front of the car. Ross had two weaknesses: women and gambling. And he handled neither very well.

Oakes opened the door and stepped out onto the open vestibule. The hot winds had full force at him here, and they plucked at his clothing and stung his flesh with sand and cinder particles. He clung to the railing as the coach swayed around a curve, waiting until it straightened before he continued. The wheel flanges screamed against the rails, and the friction of the brakes heated the metal shoes. He caught the strong smell of hot, tortured metal.

He opened the door of the coach ahead and saw Mrs. Lowden, sitting by herself. She was a pretty little thing with no great depth behind her eyes. What did a man do with a woman like that after his few moments' interest in her were over? An amused shine was in her eyes as she returned his look, and he suspected she guessed he was looking for Ross. He frowned at her, and she made a moue at him, then laughed. He passed her, knowing a small relief. At least Ross wasn't with her.

He found Ross three coaches ahead. Ross stared out of the window, and Oakes studied him before he spoke. It wasn't hard to understand why women were attracted to him. He had Oakes's height but was built on more slender lines, and his features were finely carved and regular. He was too good-looking, and it could be a weakness in a man. His black hair was thick and glossy, lying in waves. Oakes had seen Josie run her fingers through it many times. Ross's nose was hawklike, thin and high-bridged. His lips were full and sensual under a thin line of black mustache. Where most men wore their mustaches full and brushlike, he kept his trimmed to a slender thread. It made a startling contrast to his even white teeth whenever he smiled or laughed. If he had an apparent facial flaw, it may have been the tendency of his eyes to shift too readily.

Some of the old childhood scenes flashed through Oakes's mind. A love for a man was built on shared experiences, and the blood tie made it even stronger. He was aware of Ross's faults, just as Ross could probably recount the list of his. Ross was a vain man, not always stable, and at times downright weak, but he was Oakes's brother. To Oakes, that expressed it simply but well. He hadn't been quite truthful to Josie. He had come out here because he couldn't bear for the bond between him and his brother to be shattered by distance.

He poked Ross's shoulder. "Josie's alone."

Ross threw him an impatient glance. His forehead was beaded with sweat, and while it was hot in the car, it wasn't hot enough to bring out moisture on an inactive man. "Tell her I'll be back in a little bit."

Oakes had seen Ross sweat like this before. It always came from some emotional stress. He forced Ross to meet his eyes. "What is it, Ross?"

"Nothing, goddamn it. Can't I do anything without you dogging my steps?"

His voice carried over the clatter of the wheels, and heads turned to look at them. Ross lowered his voice. "I'm only waiting for someone."

Oakes sat down beside him. "Then I'll wait with you."

Color gathered in Ross's face, and his eyes grew murky with passion. Oakes expected an outburst, but Ross kept it bottled.

The train was slowing, and Oakes thrust his head out of the window. They were coming into a station, a water tank beside it, surrounded by a cluster of frame houses stripped of paint by the wind and burned to a drab grayness by the sun. The handful of buildings was hardly large enough to be graced by a name, and Oakes didn't bother to look for it. He had seen too many of these drab little stations dotted throughout the trip. The engine would be here only long enough to refuel and water.

Without the opposition of the clatter of the wheels, a hum of conversation rose in the car. Oakes kept his voice low. "Are you waiting for a woman?"

"Damn it!"

Oakes's fingers closed on his arm. Ross winced and lowered his voice. "I'm not waiting for a woman."

"I'll see."

They sat in stubborn silence until the train picked up speed again. The sweating was more pronounced on Ross's forehead.

"Maybe he's not coming back," Oakes heard him mutter. He stabbed him with his eyes. "Who?"

Ross pulled at his fingers. "Delaney."

"The gambler?" Oakes's anger was evident. Delaney was a little man with a sharpness of feature and manner. For three nights Oakes had watched him deal monte, faro, and poker. He would bet his last dollar that Delaney was crooked.

The answer was written in Ross's harassed eyes. "He promised to come back and let me get even. I was wearing out my string of bad luck."

Oakes knew a furious impulse to hit him. "You damned fool. How much did he take you for?"

Ross could barely get the words out. "Two hundred dollars."

The wild anger swelled in Oakes. He wished Josie had heard that. Then he wanted to hear her say Ross was no baby who needed looking after.

He jumped to his feet, and Ross followed him. He caught Oakes at the end of the coach. "You're not going to tell Josie?"

For a moment this face was totally strange to Oakes. He curbed his rage with effort. "I'm going to find Delaney and get your money back." He would, if he had to beat it out of the man. "Now get out of my way."

Ross stepped meekly aside. Oakes didn't look at him again. He went through four cars, and Delaney was in none of them. But he had to be somewhere on this train.

The conductor blocked his way in the next car. The brakeman was behind him, a burly man with a massive neck so short it looked as though his head were set in his shoulders. His face was red and coarse-featured, and his eyes held a hungry shine. The shine said he remembered the derailed engine and Oakes's display of strength. Physical prowess meant everything to this man. He wouldn't be happy until he tested his own against Oakes's.

The conductor scowled at him. "What are you storming through the cars for?"

"Where's Delaney?"

"You won't find him on the train." Both conductor and brakeman enjoyed Oakes's rage.

Oakes remembered the brief stop at the drab little station, and understood. The conductor was right. He wouldn't find Delaney on this train. Delaney had fleeced his sheep to his estimate of his capacity. He would wait at the station and catch another train—east or west bound—it wouldn't matter to Delaney.

Oakes cursed himself for being slow-witted. The setup was so plain now. "You gave him protection while he worked the train. How much did he split with you?"

The conductor's eyes sharpened. Oakes had hit close to the truth. The brakie's words confirmed it. "Mister, you've got a fat mouth."

The conductor's outflung arm stopped his move. "Easy, Jack." His eyes never left Oakes's face. "If you think you have a complaint, make it at the division office in Sacramento. You'll have ample time. We change engines there." He shoved brusquely past Oakes.

"Don't think I won't." Somewhere in a company as big as this railroad there was an honest man, a man who would listen to him.

Jack thrust his face into Oakes's. "That mouth is going to get you into trouble."

Oakes's fists bunched, and the conductor called, "Come on, Jack."

Jack moved reluctantly to join him, and Oakes let him go. A brawl wouldn't get Ross's money back. Maybe nothing would.

He walked back to his car, where he found Ross talking and laughing with Josie. Her eyes shone, and her face was absorbed. It was small wonder that she loved him. When Ross wanted to use that captivating charm, he could enthrall anybody. In the long run, Oakes was sure his brother loved Josie. What Oakes couldn't understand was how Ross could set that love aside for momentary diversions.

He sat down across from them, keeping his lips clamped lest accusing words spill out on Ross. He caught Josie's weighing glances. She was comparing his sullen mood to Ross's gay one, and it could only be an unfavorable comparison. It did nothing to calm Oakes's anger. He sat there and let it build all the way to Sacramento.

He was first off the train when it stopped before the wooden station at the foot of K Street. He heard Josie call his name, but he didn't turn his head. He strode into the small, bare building, his anger unabated. Somebody was going to listen to him. A ticket counter filled one end of the room. A pot-bellied stove was in the center of the room, and the walls were lined with hard, uninviting-looking benches.

A stoop-shouldered man with a sour face was behind the counter. He wore a green eyeshade and black sleeve protectors, and he watched Oakes approach with bored eyes.

Oakes spread his palms flat on the counter. He towered a good six inches over the clerk. "I want to see the head man."

"What about?"

Oakes bristled at the insolence in the question. "That's my business."

The clerk knew an indignant passenger when he saw one. He grinned slyly as he reached for a pencil and sheet of paper. "If it's a complaint, fill out this form."

Oakes stared at the form, then lifted his eyes. "What happens to it after I fill it out?"

"That's our business, mister. Now, don't bother me anymore."

He started to turn away, and Oakes reached across the counter and grabbed him. He hauled him up against the counter's edge, hearing the man's shirt rip in the process. "Don't be turning your back on me. You'll throw no complaint of mine in the wastebasket. Are you going to call the boss for me?"

The clerk looked into the angry eyes so near his own and gulped. Then the frightened look faded. "Take your hands off me."

Something had happened to change the man's attitude from fright to bravado. Oakes turned his head. Jack was coming toward the counter, and his face was eager. Three men were behind him, and they all carried the same stamp of anticipation. It wasn't hard to figure them as railroad employees. Oakes let go of the clerk and put his back against the counter. The station was filling with passengers. It wasn't the place he would have picked for this, but it couldn't be avoided. Only the throbbing of the veins at his temples showed his tension.

Jack bared his teeth. "I told you that fat mouth would get you in trouble. You'll learn you can't come in here and manhandle any of us."

Oakes threw out a pacifying hand. "There's no trouble. We were just talking."

The clerk swore. "Talking? Look at my shirt."

Jack thought he had a frightened man before him, and his lip curled. The sneer wasn't wholly set on his face when Oakes slugged him. He hit him hard but a little high. His knuckles split lips and pulled a spurt of blood, and there were probably loosened teeth after the blow. But it was too high to be a knockout.

Jack stumbled backward, his arms flailing for balance, a stunned surprise on his face. He wobbled into two of the men behind him, and they kept him from going down.

A woman screamed, and feet scurried toward

the door as people tried to get out of the station. Oakes plowed forward, and his lowered shoulder was an awesome force, catching Jack in the face and knocking him and the two men to the floor. They went down in a welter of waving, twisting arms and legs, and the tangle caught Oakes's legs and knocked them from under him.

As he went down, the man remaining on his feet aimed a kick at his head. A boot sole scraped along Oakes's cheek, tearing away skin and drawing blood. The sting of it broke the final binding of Oakes's anger.

Arms pulled at him, trying to hold him down, and a foot was hooked across the back of his knee. He came to his feet, hauling up two of them with him. Somebody rained blows at the back of his head, and he didn't feel them. He grabbed a clinging man and jerked him loose. He pitched him at one of the benches and heard its splintering ruin. He used his fist like a mallet, hitting the second man on top of the head. It drove the man to the floor, and his arms fell away from Oakes's waist.

Oakes stood on braced legs drawing deeply on his laboring lungs. His cheek oozed blood, and his shirt hung in tatters. The red mist of rage blinded him. One man lay on the floor, but three of them were on their feet, or getting up. He waited until they converged upon him from three directions. He roared and picked up a bench, swinging it like a flail. The end of it caught Jack in the chest, knocking him across the room. He slammed into the wall, pounding the breath from himself. He slid to the floor, a stupefied expression on his face.

Oakes swung the bench again. He knocked the pot-bellied stove from its legs, and it hit the floor with a metallic crash, bouncing and clattering. His head was full of a roaring noise, and somebody kept up a high-pitched screaming that tore at his nerves. The doorway was full of people, and he wasn't sure they were trying to get in or out. It could be reinforcements coming, and he didn't even blink. He didn't give a damn if the whole railroad poured in through that door.

He waved them toward him with a huge arm. "Come on. All of you."

He didn't see the man with the badge slip quickly through the rear door. He didn't see the gun barrel descend against the back of his head, nor did he feel it. The blackness came suddenly, and its hold was complete.

Chapter Two

Oakes came out of the courtroom, a dazed expression on his face. The anger would come later, but for the moment he was too stunned to think. He passed a group of men, and one of them made a jeering remark. Oakes didn't even hear it.

"Two hundred dollars," he muttered. "Two hundred dollars."

He shook his head, and the gesture was unwise for it started a dull throb of pain in his head. That lawman had really hit him yesterday evening.

The strong morning sunlight was harsh to his aching head. He crossed the street to a restaurant and stepped inside. As yet the growing heat hadn't driven out the night's coolness, and the shadowy interior was welcome. He moved to a table and sat down, grunting as he did so. With less restraint, the grunt could have been a groan.

At a waitress's inquiring look, Oakes said, "Coffee. Lots of it."

Her eyes added up his size, and a flash of knowledge shone in her eyes. "Oh, you're the big one they had on trial this morning."

She smiled at his bristling. "I'm not taking sides against you." Her face was hard with the knowledge of living learned at too great a cost, and the morning light wasn't kind to her. She looked as though all the pity had been pounded out of her, including any for herself. "I'm not taking sides against the railroad, either. Nobody does that."

"I did."

She shook her head. "I wish you luck, mister. If you keep on the way you're going, you're going to need all you can get. I'll bring your coffee."

She swished her hips as she moved away, and Oakes observed the movement without interest.

She brought a pot of coffee and a cup to the table, and Oakes paid, and thanked her with a nod. Two hundred dollars! Added to what Ross lost, it made an appalling sum. At the moment the figure was a high wall, and his thoughts couldn't clamber over it.

He was on his third cup of coffee when the man approached his table. He was on the small side and dressed in city clothes. He wore a hard hat and a bright red vest and cloth-topped buttoned shoes. His brown mustache was bushy, partially breaking the thin lines of a cynical mouth. His face was foxlike in its sharpness, and those bright round eyes missed little.

"Mind if I sit down?" He was seated before he finished the request. He grinned at the heat starting in Oakes's eyes. "Don't boil at me. I'm on your side." His grin broadened at the gathering storm in Oakes's face. He should have been intimidated by it, but apparently his smallness didn't extend to his courage.

"I was in the station when you started the riot." He nodded in admiration. "You did what a lot of people have wanted to do for a long time. You stood up and broke a few railroad heads."

His sincerity was obvious, and Oakes's suspicions thawed. "A lot of good it did me. I woke up in jail with an aching head."

The little man laughed. "They must have had a hell of a time dragging you there."

He had somebody to talk to, and Oakes needed that. "Were you at the trial?" At the man's nod, Oakes's face darkened. "That was no trial. The judge wouldn't even listen to me. That railroad lawyer turned everything I said around." His face burned at the memory of his treatment. The courtroom had been filled with the jeering faces of the lying witnesses.

"You did start it."

Oakes's frown returned. "I hit him a split second before he was ready to swing on me."

"Sure. But they used it against you. Your case was lost the minute you touched railroad property."

"Two hundred dollars," Oakes said bleakly. "For the fine and damages. The whole damned building isn't worth that much."

The little man grinned. "You tore it up pretty good. I talked to your brother and his wife before the train pulled out yesterday. He said they couldn't do anything for you here, and he didn't want to lose the fare. They want you to join them in Starvation Valley."

Oakes scowled. "Starvation Valley?"

"Weren't you headed for the railroad land in Tulare County? That's Starvation Valley."

"Who are you?" Oakes demanded.

"Galen Mundro." The little man waited for the name to register, then said with mock disappointment, "That's fame for you. A man writes a few pieces and expects his name to be well known."

"Are you a writer?"

"A reporter. The San Francisco *Examiner*. Against everything the railroad stands for." Mundro leaned forward, a hot glow in his eyes. "I hate the men who own and run it. I hit them with words, and it doesn't bother them any more than a few gnats bother a bull. I've had the feeling for some time that one of these days a man like you would come along. A big man, a physical man who could only be shoved so far before he shoved back. A man big and tough enough that the little man would rally around him. You may be that man."

Oakes shook his head. "I'm a farmer. You picked the wrong man. I didn't do so well against them last night or again this morning." A thought struck him. "Does the railroad own that judge?"

"They do. They own a lot of the legislators here in Sacramento. They own city and county officials. They own the Railroad Commission, the men who fix the rates the way the railroad tells them to fix them. Their only standard is 'all the traffic will bear.'"

"And you're looking for one man to stand against that much power?"

"One man to be a starting point. One rock that cannot be washed away."

Oakes fingered the lump on his head. "I've had one brush with them. That's enough." His eyes narrowed. "Why are you so damned interested, anyway?"

Mundro gave him a mocking grin. "Why, I'll get the biggest story of the decade." His face sobered. "And maybe reestablish my belief that the little man doesn't always have to lose."

Oakes thought those were light reasons to push a man into an all-out fight. He started to rise. "I can't do you any good."

"Wait." Mundro's face had completely changed. It had a malevolent twist, and the eyes burned bright. "Maybe this will make you understand. My father was a farmer. I still remember his scraping to send me to school."

Oakes stirred uneasily. He didn't know this man well enough to exchange confidences.

"Then he took up land in Starvation Valley. He was tough. Nobody pushed him around. If he couldn't push back, he talked about it—to the wrong people. He was found dead one morning. Beaten by person or persons unknown."

He endured Oakes's study. "I'm not lying."

Oakes decided he wasn't. "You want me to find who killed him?"

"The trail's too old and too well covered. I was down there." Mundro's shrug spoke of his failure. "But you might prevent it from happening to somebody else. Are you going to lose anything by talking to me?"

"I guess not." Oakes settled back in his chair. Besides, there wouldn't be another train south until this evening, and the thought of taking his aching head out into that pitiless sun was too much.

"You believe the railroad was behind your father's death?"

"I know it." Mundro pressed the ball of his thumb against the table and turned it. "They smash all opposition, just like that. Everybody was for the railroad during its building. It took men of vision to build it, to give California a transcontinental link. Four men made forty million dollars apiece out of the building. But that wasn't enough. It turned them into hogs. And like hogs they're eating everything in sight." He ticked off the names on the fingers of his left hand. "Huntington, Stanford, Hopkins, and Crocker. A giant four-fingered hand squeezing the blood out of everything it touches. Do you know the freight rates from New York to San Francisco are less than the rates from San Francisco to Fresno? The shorter haul is all Central Pacific lines, and they can fix the rates they want. The railroad demands and gets the right of examining a man's books. If his profit is more than they thought, his shipping rates are raised. They've crushed wool growers, miners, and fruit raisers. I could tell you how they've wrecked the lemon industry, how it's that way with everything they get their hands on."

Oakes shook his head. "Everything you say may be true. But I don't see where any of it touches me."

"Good God! Are you blind? It started touching you the moment you stepped on that train. You didn't like its touch, or you wouldn't have gotten in trouble. It's your fight, it's the fight of every man who came out on that train with you. You're planning on taking up land in Tulare County. Railroad land, for most of the government land is gone. The government sold its land outright, the railroad only promises to sell. And on that vague promise you'll work that land, you'll improve it." He shook his head in a weary gesture. "The railroad will profit by your improvements. Not you."

Oakes stared thoughtfully toward the front of the room. Mundro wasn't doing him any good cramming these thoughts into his head. His eyes touched a tall man, standing at the counter. Mundro had made no effort to keep his voice down, and Oakes was suddenly aware that the tall man had been following their conversation for some time. He frowned at the man and received an amused smile in return.

Mundro sighed. "I guess I couldn't expect this to reach you. Maybe I am in it because of my father's memory." His voice lowered until it was barely audible. "And maybe I'm sick unto death of all the little men, like my father, amounting to nothing."

Oakes's face was troubled as he hunted for words. He could understand what pushed Mundro, but it still wasn't his fight. He held what he had in mind to say, as he saw the tall man approaching their table. The man stopped across from Mundro and stared at him. He was well barbered and well tailored, and a look of softness was about him. That was superficial, for the eyes were cold and hard.

Those eyes fixed Mundro. "Friend, you talk too much. It can be a bad habit."

Oakes flared. "No one asked you for your opinion."

The cold eyes swung to Oakes. "And you, my friend, learn very hard. I should think one lesson would have been enough for you." He turned abruptly and walked out of the restaurant.

Oakes glared after him. "Who was that?"

Mundro shook his head. "He probably works for them." His eyes held a new brightness. "He struck fire from you. Perhaps I wasn't wrong in thinking you are the man."

"You were wrong. I'm looking for no fight." Oakes stood and thrust out his hand. "Thanks for the talk, Mr. Mundro."

The old cynical grin was back on Mundro's lips. "I'll be seeing you again. I'm coming down to Starvation Valley soon. Maybe I'm curious to see how much men will take before they hit back."

Oakes nodded and walked toward the door. He stopped and looked back. A strange little man but a likable one. A lot like a conscience, Oakes thought, with the stinging ability to make a man feel uncomfortable. He raised his hand in a gesture of farewell. He doubted that he would talk to Galen Mundro again.

He spent a long and weary day waiting for the evening train south. When a man knew no one in a city, it was hard to pass the time. He could only eat so much, and he could only drink so much. He walked through the capitol grounds looking soberly at the capitol. Justice for all men was supposed to come from under that dome. But somehow it always seemed to get choked off. He stared at the dome, remembering what Mundro had said, and his feeling of frustration and futility grew. He shook his head, pushing the thoughts out of his mind.

He was at the station an hour before train time, and the boy found him in the waiting room. "Mr. Paulson?" At Oakes's nod, the boy said, "He was right. He said to pick the biggest man I found here, and he'd be the right one."

"Who was right?"

"Mr. Mundro. He's in the hospital. Hurt real bad. He wants to see you."

Oakes gripped the boy's arm. "Take me there."

It was three blocks to the small white building, and Oakes made the pace so fast the boy didn't have breath left to talk. No, he didn't know what kind of an accident Mr. Mundro had been in.

At the hospital, Oakes pulled a quarter from his pocket and handed it to the youngster.

The boy bounced it in his hand. "Mr. Mundro gave me a dollar."

"Then you've been well paid."

The boy tried to look indignant under those sardonic eyes and failed. "Yes," he admitted, and grinned.

Oakes shoved the youngster's hair down over his eyes. This one would make out in life.

He stepped inside and asked directions to Mundro's room. The nurse was rushed, and she was impatient with Oakes's questions. "A fight, I think. He can tell you."

He walked into Mundro's room and stopped

short, appalled at what he saw. Mundro's face was a mass of bruises. His lips were broken and swollen, and one eye was tightly shut.

Oakes kept his voice low, though he felt like yelling. "What happened?"

Mundro attempted to shift position and winced. "They got some ribs, too. I think our tall friend in the restaurant is responsible. I thought I was followed when I went to the capitol. They waylaid me in an alley. I couldn't put up too much of a fight against four of them. I guess they stomped me after they knocked me out."

"But why?"

Mundro's good eye gleamed. "They don't like criticism. Even from a single voice."

But a loud and strident one, Oakes thought. It had been picking at him all day. "Would you know them? Maybe I can find them."

"It happened too hard and fast. I didn't get a clear look at any of them."

"They could've killed you."

"No, just a beating to make me more careful of what I say and write."

Oakes stared at him. "Why did you send for me? I can't help you—" He stopped as the answer formed in his mind. "Hah! You wanted me to see this. You figured it would work on me."

"Hasn't it?" Mundro made a bad job of his attempt to grin with his broken lips.

"It has not. I'm going to catch that train. I've

got my own business to attend to, and it's going to keep me too busy to look after anybody else's."

He stalked to the door and looked back. "You get yourself another horse to bridle."

Mundro was still trying to smile, and that infuriated Oakes even more. He was sorry that Mundro had been beaten. A man had a right to voice an opinion without fear of physical attack. He stepped out into the corridor. He would remember that bruised face for a long time. Damn Galen Mundro, anyway.

Chapter Three

The San Joaquin Valley was an immense flat plain stretching in emptiness as far as the eye could see. Only along the rivers and occasional streams was there any green, and to a man used to the lush summertime greenness of Ohio, this drab vista struck with appalling force. The vegetation was thin and scraggly, its limp foliage a harsh, dull, metallic green. Oakes could name none of the plants he saw, but there were not enough of them to begin to cover the ground. The use of "ground" was a kindness to this soil. He had scooped up a handful of it and let it trickle through his fingers, thinking in dismay, It's pure sand. And this was the land that was supposed to feed and shelter them.

He left the train at Fresno and asked at the station for information about the train that carried Ross and Josie.

"What number was it?"

The clerk's tone was brusque, but Oakes swallowed his resentment. Sacramento was too fresh in his mind. "I don't know. But it was supposed to stop here yesterday morning. My family was on it."

The clerk's shrug was indifferent. "Maybe they got off here. Maybe they went on. If they're not in Fresno, they might be in Goshen or Tulare or Kingsburg. Or maybe Tipton or Hanford." His grin held a touch of malice. "Ask at any of those places."

He turned away, and Oakes's hands itched to pull him back. He stomped out of the station. Mundro's mocking smile came to mind. So far, Mundro was right. It seemed that the smallest dealings with the railroad made a man mad.

He stepped out onto the street, and the Fresno sun hit him with the impact of a club. The heat wrapped around him like a stifling blanket, making him feel as though he wanted to pant against it. How could anything grow in such heat and in sand instead of soil?

Fresno wasn't a large town, but there seemed to be a pulsating quality about it. Oakes had noticed that when a town had this feeling it never stayed small. Even in this heat there was movement on the street, and the stores seemed well stocked. Oakes asked for Josie and Ross at three hotels and received negative answers. The desk clerk at the last one was an old man and talkative. He rubbed a handkerchief over his bald head. "They tell you a man doesn't notice the heat out here. Don't you believe it."

"I'm noticing it."

"The nights are cool, though. A man can stand the heat, if he can get his sleep."

Oakes grunted. That was the first advantage he

had heard for this land. The overhead fan needed greasing. It made a squeaky sound as it listlessly stirred the hot air.

The old man shook his head. "It's going to be tough finding your family. You didn't have a definite town to go to?"

Oakes muttered a soft oath. That was Ross's brilliant idea. They would look the towns over as they passed through them. He shook his head.

"The railroad wouldn't try to help you?" The old man read the answer on Oakes's face. "That's typical. They want you people out here, they need you to fill up this emptiness, then they treat you like cattle. It's a big gamble when people pull up stakes, leave land they know, and come out to something like this. Maybe they'll win, though." His tone put a dubious reflection on his words.

"If my family's not at any of the hotels, where would they be most likely to be?"

"Most of the emigrants don't stop at hotels. They stay on the cars until they get their land. I heard the sidings at Fresno are full. Your train probably went on south." He fingered his lower lip. "Goshen, Tulare, Hanford. They might be at any one of them. If I were you, I'd get me a horse and stop at every station. You'll find them."

Oakes said an appreciative thanks. He asked directions to a livery stable, and the old man said, "Take it easy. This heat can kill a man when he's not used to it."

Oakes nodded and stepped outside. The searing sunlight made him squinch his eyelids against it. He hated to spend the money now for a horse, but if he chose wisely it wouldn't be wasted. He would pick a heavy-boned, big-footed animal, one that could be used for plowing.

He passed a house at the head of the second block and retraced his steps, his eyes wide in disbelief. That was a patch of real grass in the yard, and geraniums and hydrangea bushes grew against the porch. The geraniums were six feet tall, a riot of red blossoms, and the hydrangeas were not far behind, each of the blossoms as big as a head of cabbage.

Oakes had never seen such flowers. Surely a different soil had been carted in here. That sand he had picked up would grow nothing like this.

He glanced around, and no one was in sight. He crossed the small yard and picked up a handful of soil at the foot of one of the geraniums. He rubbed it through his fingers, and it was sand but now moist and because of it a different color and texture. But it couldn't be the same sand. Something had been added to it.

A fat woman with a round, happy face came out on the porch. "I didn't believe it either, mister, when I first saw it." She waved Oakes's apologies away. "It's all right. I'm proud of my flowers. Come around in back, and I'll show you gladioli like you never saw before."

Oakes followed her around the house. A row of gladioli grew along the back of the house, high enough to reach halfway up the windows. He loved growing things, and he could appreciate the long flowering spikes with their burdens of huge blossoms.

"What did you add to the sand?"

"Just water." Her laugh rang out at his expression. "I know it's hard to believe. But this sand is rich. Add water, and it'll grow anything. Oh, the buckets of water I've carried. But it's worth it."

"Where do you get the water?"

"From deep wells. And irrigation ditches." She swept out an arm. "Ditches that bring the water from the mountains. You should see the places where the water has reached. Orchards and vineyards, gardens and crops. You can grow anything. Only faster and bigger than anywhere else. Are you thinking of buying land?"

Oakes nodded.

"Don't buy railroad land. The government gave them every other section for building the road, and they've got a lot of land to sell. But my husband says they can't be trusted."

Oakes grimaced. "That seems to be the popular opinion."

"Well, when there's that much smoke—" She left the sentence unfinished. "But most of the government land is gone. I wish you luck, mister." She waddled toward the door. "I can't take too much of this sun."

Oakes called a thanks after her. He looked at the yard again. A new respect for this land was in his eyes. A sleeping life was there, only waiting to be awakened with water. A new briskness was in his step, a glow of hope in his eyes.

He rode south after leaving Fresno. His mount was a heavy-footed animal more suited to the plow than to a rider. But that qualification was uppermost when Oakes bought the horse, and he was content with it.

He followed the twin ribbons of sun-heated steel through the emptiness. At times he would ride for several hours without seeing sign of human life. When he did pass a house, it was a crude, makeshift affair of rough boards, the sun slowly beating the yellow new color from them. They were not encouraging sights. Most of the barns in Ohio were better than these so-called houses. The elation he had felt in Fresno was fading. This was the same land, but the water was so terribly far from it.

He stopped at Kingsburg, Tulare, and Tipton. Kingsburg and Tulare were bustling towns, and he speculated on what could be stored in the huge warehouses there. Surely they were built to handle some kind of crop, but what crop would give bountifully enough to fill a warehouse that size? The sidings were filled with lines of emigrant cars, and Oakes patiently rode down them. Anger increased in him at the way these people were handled: shunted onto sidings like cattle to await somebody's whim. He listened to crying, complaining children, looked at women growing haggard and big-eyed under the heat, and his wrath grew. Waiting was hard when there was no definite end of it in sight. One hour ran into another, and the despair grew in direct proportion to the string of hours.

It took him four days, but he found the train he wanted on a siding at Hanford. The desert stretched on all sides, pitting its silent, passive resistance against man's efforts. But here and there, there was a patch of green. Someone had found water, someone had found a way to beat that passive resistance.

He rode along the cars, seeing people he knew. Some greeted him with an attempt at cheerfulness, others were too beaten down to care. The waiting was stamping its mark on them.

Josie stood in the doorway of their car, and her eyes were turned far away. Something close to panic was trying to take over her face. It seemed a year since he had seen her, and all his feelings were in his voice as he said, "Hello, Josie."

She turned her head, and he was sure her face would crumble. She tried to say it gaily, but she couldn't keep the bitterness from cropping out.

"Welcome home, Oakes."

Chapter Four

He wished he could put his arms about her, and he wouldn't trust himself to say more than her name. He kept his face turned from her as he dismounted, for the flood of feeling was a treacherous thing and would surely show. He finally looked at her and smiled. "I was detained a little."

She tried to be severe, but her relief at seeing him broke the edges off her words. "You lost your temper again." Her lip corners quivered, and she couldn't control her laughter. "You wrecked that station."

He made a wry expression. "They came at me first, Josie."

"I wanted to stay. But Ross said there was nothing we could do for you. He thought it best we get here as quickly as possible. Was it bad?"

"A bump on the head. And a small fine. That's all, Josie."

He looked at the cars on the siding and frowned. "Have you been in this car since you got here?"

Her lips had a suspicious tremble. "The railroad is slow about giving us our land, Oakes."

His eyes darkened. This shadeless siding was a hell during the day hours.

"It hasn't been too bad." She spoke too hastily.

"And as Ross says, it costs us nothing to live here."

He stared steadily at her. "Where is Ross?"

"In town. Trying to get our land."

Her haste at saying it aroused his suspicions. "How long has he been gone?"

"Since this morning."

He thought that was probably a lie, too. She was lying to keep him from getting mad at Ross.

"I'll go see if I can help him." Her lying wasn't going to work.

Her "Oakes" checked him. He turned a set face toward her. She couldn't talk him out of his anger at Ross this time. Ross had been gone longer than since this morning. Perhaps he had been gone last night, or even a couple of nights. It wouldn't be beyond Ross's way of doing things.

"Is—is it good land, Oakes?"

So that was what troubled her most. Her faltering question expressed all the dismaying doubt she felt about this barren country.

"It's good land, Josie. Rich land. I've seen what it can grow. It needs water. It's going to be all right, Josie," he finished gently.

He mounted and looked at her. She seemed so lonely and alone, standing in the doorway of that car. He lifted his hand, and she returned his salute. His anger was coming to a boil. Damn Ross for leaving her like this.

Hanford was a dusty, hot little town, with

the rawness of new building everywhere. The buildings were thrown-up affairs, for the paramount problem on men's minds was wresting a living from this land; not shelter. The business district wasn't over three blocks long. He passed the post office, several saloons, and a general store. A large, square building, occupying half a block, advertised hay and grain. The gnawed tie racks were well filled. Saddle horses stood next to heavy draft animals. Buggies, buckboards, and wagons were jammed close together, and animals and vehicles were covered with the gray dust of this country.

There was life here, a stirring against the seed pod, a wanting to break out and expand, and Oakes felt its presence. It put an itch in him, a need to get started. He forced his attention on the immediate business. Where would be the best place to start looking for Ross? Most likely the saloons.

An old Mexican, barefooted and wearing ragged white trousers, crossed the street ahead of him, and Oakes stopped his horse, not wanting to put any pressure on the shuffling, unsure steps of the old man.

He heard the clatter of wheels and the pound of hooves before the vehicle came into view. A light buggy careened around the corner, the bay horse in its shafts in full run. The old man threw up his head, and for a frightening moment Oakes thought he was going to freeze in the middle of the street. Oakes yelled a warning, and the old man responded with surprising alacrity. He made a bound for the safety of the walk, and the horse brushed and half spun him. Only a hasty grab at a hitching rail saved the old man from going down. He hung there, his face twisted with rage as he shouted maledictions at the buggy's driver.

Oakes was wheeling his horse as the buggy passed him. The woman driving it was in trouble. Her mouth was open wide, either in screaming for help, or in fearful crying. He couldn't be sure. She was by him too soon, the quickness of her passing distorting impressions. He had a hazy picture of jet-black hair streaming in the wind and of her frantic, useless sawing on the reins.

He was a quarter block behind before he got his horse into full motion, and he had grave doubts of the animal ever overtaking the runaway bay. His heels drummed on its flanks, demanding what speed it had. As the last building fell behind him, he thought he might be gaining a little.

Slowly, he drew up on the buggy. He prayed the vehicle wouldn't hit a rock or a rut in the road and overturn, and he prayed the woman had enough sense not to stand in the careening, jolting buggy. He was surprised at the way his horse narrowed the gap between it and the buggy. Either his horse had greater foot than he had thought, or the bay didn't live up to its lines. Before a mile was covered he was abreast the buggy, and he shouted encouragement to its occupant. It was queer, but up close she didn't seem frightened, and she called something he didn't catch.

He drew even with the bay and heard its heavy, labored breathing. Gouts of foam flew from its muzzle, and one of them splashed against his cheek. Its withers and flanks were blackened and moist from its sweating, and it was hard to believe this short a run could put the animal in such distress. It had to have been running long before he saw it, or it had little bottom.

He leaned over and seized its bridle, taking care not to jerk its head too quickly. He stayed in the saddle, using his heavier horse as a brake, and in a hundred yards dragged the bay to a stop. He sprang out of the saddle, still holding onto the bridle. He had expected more resistance, for a runaway horse didn't calm too readily. This one didn't even throw its head. It stood on wide spread legs, its head hanging low, its barrel heaving.

He looked at the woman. "Are you all right?"

Her lips were slightly parted, and for an instant he thought the reaction to fear had frozen her tongue. She was a disturbingly beautiful woman, somewhere in her middle twenties. Her eyes were almond-shaped and slightly tilted, giving her an enigmatic look. He had the odd feeling those eyes were evaluating him, and that didn't fit the circumstances at all. Her mouth was full and red, and the disarray of her thick black hair added rather than detracted from her appearance. There was Spanish influence somewhere along her background, for it showed in the color of her hair and in the suggestion of olive duskiness in her complexion. She wore a lawn skirt and a shirtwaist, and his eyes were drawn to the woman fullness in the latter garment. He realized he was staring and hastily lifted his eyes. An odd shine was in her eyes, and her lips were beginning to quirk. This woman wasn't frightened now, and he doubted that she had been.

He couldn't quite understand what was happening, and it put a frown on his face. He asked again, "Are you all right?"

Her lips trembled and broke into laughter. Her laughter deepened, and her parted lips showed perfect white teeth.

His face colored, and he couldn't keep the edge out of his voice. "What's so funny?"

"You. How gallant you were. Did you think you were saving me from a runaway horse? Why, you fool. I never saw a horse I couldn't control."

His face froze with outrage. He knew now that the bay had been running before he saw it, and that explained why his horse could overtake it.

"Do you know you almost ran down an old man back there?"

She shrugged gracefully. As casually as that

she discarded the thought of possible injury to the old Mexican; and with it went her sense of responsibility or blame.

It increased his outrage. "Somebody didn't teach you to think about other people. Maybe it isn't too late."

Her eyes turned hot and smoky, and she grabbed up her whip. "Would you like to try it now?"

If he made a move she would slash him with the whip. That wasn't his deterrent. But to stop her from using it he would have to manhandle her, and the thought didn't set well. He let his eyes flick over her face. "It's not my job, nor worth my time."

As he mounted he heard her laugh again. That last remark had salvaged him little. He whirled his horse and looked at her. He shook his head, making it the most disparaging gesture he could.

It only increased her laughter and put more taunting in her face. "I'll look forward to seeing you again."

"Not if I can avoid it." He kicked his horse into motion. He felt futile and foolish, and a man was helpless under either. A pampered, useless woman. He couldn't get the fullness of that shirt-waist out of his mind. Not completely useless, he thought, and a wry grin moved his lips.

His search for Ross didn't sweeten his humor. He finally found him in the Lady Gay Saloon, and he wasn't surprised to see him at a poker table. He grunted at the sizable stack of chips before his brother. At least Ross didn't appear to be losing.

Oakes touched him on the shoulder. Ross looked at him, and for an instant no recognition showed in his eyes. He always looked wild and distraught when the gambling fever had him.

"Let's go, Ross."

Resentment twisted Ross's face. "Damn it, Oakes. I'm riding a winning streak."

"It's a good time to stop, then. Cash them in."

Six other men were at the table, and one of them made a feeble attempt at humor. "Wiley, are you going to let him walk away from your table a winner?"

The breadth of Wiley's shoulders made him look misshapen. He wore a green eyeshade and wicker sleeve protectors. His shirt was the finest linen, and the black tie was a fine, crisp line. Some past force had broken his nose, and it hadn't set properly. That crooked nose dominated his face.

He locked eyes with Oakes. "You're interrupting the game." Those slate-gray eyes didn't waver. He had successfully known and handled violence before.

"Did you have him all set up to take him?"

Wiley's eyes turned wicked as faint color touched his sallow complexion. He stood and came around the table. "I hate to have to do this, friend." He rushed Oakes before the sentence was finished.

Oakes held until the last split second, then sidestepped. Wiley's swinging fist fanned his cheek. He threw out a foot, and Wiley stumbled over it. He brought his arm down in a clubbing swing, smashing Wiley across the shoulders with it. Wiley's momentum carried him on, and the force of Oakes's blow pushed him downward. He went for a few broken steps, his torso parallel to the floor, before he lost his balance. He crashed to the floor and slid, the boards burning his cheek.

Oakes's eyes blazed at Ross. "Pick up your chips."

"Look out," somebody shouted, and Oakes whirled.

The force of Wiley's fall had spilled the derringer from its hiding place, and it lay in front of him. His cheek was bleeding, his eyes dazed, but he was reaching for the gun.

Oakes jumped for him, his right boot coming down just as Wiley's hand closed on the gun. He stamped the hand hard, and Wiley's outcry rose high and shrill. His eyes were wild as he jerked his hand from the floor. He held it by the wrist and shook it, and blood flew from the mashed fingers.

Oakes grabbed Wiley by the shirtfront and

yanked him to his feet. "I ought to break your neck for that. Now, cash his chips."

Wiley was through. He whimpered as he pulled money from a pocket with his left hand. The right hand dripped blood onto the table.

Oakes looked at Ross. "Does that tally?" At Ross's nod, he picked up the sheaf of bills and thrust them into his pocket. His face dared Ross to protest.

He turned Ross toward the door. Before they could move, a man stepped through it, blocking their way. His neck lapped over his collar, and his belly hung over his belt. He had nervous eyes and a blustering voice, but he wore a star.

"What kind of a ruckus is going on in here?" he demanded. He saw Wiley's mangled hand. "Jesus." He licked his lips, making the word almost inaudible.

"Arrest him, Henshaw," Wiley yelled. "He came in here and started trouble."

One of the onlookers shook his head. "That wasn't the way it was at all, Wiley. You rushed him first, and he knocked you down. You tried to gun him, and he stamped your hand." He grinned at Wiley's murderous eyes. "Haven't you had things your way long enough?"

Henshaw wet his lips. "Somebody had to start this trouble." He was a sorry picture as he tried to face Oakes down. "Mister, I know about you. You made trouble in Sacramento.

Now you come down here and start it here."

His knowledge had to come from a telegram, and Oakes's eyes bored into him. "So you're in the railroad's pay, too."

He caught the subtle shifting of alliance in the room. Excepting Wiley and the sheriff, these men were farmers, and Oakes's words about the railroad put them behind him.

The man who had spoken in Oakes's defense said, "Arrest him, and all of us will tell exactly how it happened."

Wiley's eyes were murderous. "I'll remember this, Ryan."

Ryan nodded. "You do that."

Oakes grinned at Henshaw's discomfort. "I'm waiting, Sheriff."

"I'm letting you go this time. But cause more trouble and you won't get off so easy next time."

His eyes slid away, and somebody snickered. The color flooded Henshaw's fat neck.

Oakes took a step toward the door. "Ross, are you coming?"

Wiley was having trouble swallowing the bitter blow to his pride. "I'll be looking for you one of these days."

"You won't have to look too hard. I expect to be around for some time."

As he went through the door he heard Wiley yell, "Get out of here, all of you. Goddamn it. Get out."

He grinned frostily. "It sounds like Wiley's in a temper."

Ross gave him a waspish glance. "Do you enjoy making enemies? First it's Wiley, then Henshaw. You'll have the whole town against us."

No, Oakes didn't enjoy making enemies. Regardless of his intentions it just happened. It seemed a man his size just naturally made a better target than a smaller one.

Chapter Five

They walked in silence for a block. "Ross, I'm glad you won." Wiley had counted out over a hundred dollars. Some of it had to be Ross's starting money, and his total winnings wouldn't be enough to cover what he had lost on the train. And certainly not enough to make up for the fine in Sacramento. But it helped.

Ross's face was sulky. "I'd have gotten it all back, if you'd stayed out of it. The cards were just beginning to come my way."

Oakes stopped short. "You played last night." He didn't have to make it a question. He could see it in Ross's eyes.

Ross wouldn't look at him. "We'd just started again when you butted in."

Oakes took a harder grip on his temper. "How much did you lose this time?"

Ross found interest in something across the street, and Oakes's fingers bit into his arm. "How much?"

"I'm over a hundred dollars in. But blame yourself for it. You broke up my winning streak."

They were out some five hundred dollars, and under the circumstances it was a frightening sum. Before when one of Ross's indiscretions was costly, there was the land to fall back upon, the dependable land with its steady promise of another crop. Here, there was nothing.

Ross jerked his arm from Oakes. "I could've won it back."

"You damned fool. Wiley's a professional, and you think you can beat him at his game. He let you win a little before he sank the hook."

His voice was gathering volume, and he stopped abruptly. If he kept on, he would be roaring at Ross. He didn't want the whole town knowing of their troubles.

"I couldn't just sit on that siding and wait, could I, Oakes?"

He had never wanted more to hit Ross. "But you can leave Josie to do that. Shut up, Ross. Just shut up."

He was going to have to tell Josie about this. Ross simply couldn't be trusted with money.

Ross thought it wise to change the subject. "I found out something about our land."

"What?" It was going to take more than a change of subject to dilute Oakes's anger.

"Dackett is the man we have to see. He's at the railroad office."

"But you didn't see him?"

"A clerk kept putting me off. He said I might see him this morning. I was going over there pretty soon." His face heated at Oakes's expression. "Damn it. I was."

"Where is this office?"

"Down the street a couple of blocks. But we can't just barge in and demand—" His words faded. Oakes was moving with long strides, and Ross hurried to catch up with him.

The look on Oakes's face worried him. "Oakes, don't get him down on us. In some things you can't just bull your way in."

Oakes put bleak eyes on him. "Should I use your way? No clerk's petty authority is going to keep me from seeing this Dackett."

"All right. Go ahead and handle it your way. You always do. But I'm not going in with you." Ross pointed out the railroad building across the street. "I'm not going to have Dackett down on me. I'll wait here for you."

"You be here when I come back." Oakes stared at him until Ross shifted his eyes. He accepted Ross's nod. After he got hard with Ross, Ross usually straightened out for a while. He put a final warning look on Ross before he crossed the street.

The railroad office was the most imposing building in town, a two storeyed affair of rough brown stone. A gold-lettered sign on the plate glass window proclaimed it to be the Railroad, Freight and Passenger Office. In smaller letters in one corner of the window were the words, "Land Office."

Ryan lounged outside the door, and Oakes stopped for a moment. "I didn't take time to thank you for speaking up for me to Henshaw."

Ryan made a deprecatory gesture. He was a gangly man, awkwardly put together, and looking all rough corners and angles. His skin was the kind that never tanned, only burned, and all summer, layer after layer of it would peel away. He had a big, loose-lipped mouth and bad teeth, but there was a quiet strength in the steady brown eyes.

"My pleasure to see Wiley taken down. Most people are afraid of him."

He commented on Oakes's grunt. "Don't take him too lightly. He won't forgive you for that mauling. That your brother you took out of the game?"

Oakes nodded.

"I thought I caught a resemblance around the mouth." He hesitated a moment. "None of my business, but your brother is a poor poker player. He can't go up against somebody like Wiley."

He grinned at Oakes's scowl. "I know. I'm butting into family business."

Oakes wanted to sting him in return. "You were playing at Wiley's table."

"Sure, and I even pick up a few dollars from the other players. But not from Wiley. I only protect myself from him. And I only sit in with a few dollars. When that's gone, I stop. I can't be hurt very bad. And that makes the big difference." A sharp appraisal was in his eyes. "Are you going to take up land here?"

The man's questions were too direct for Oakes's taste, and it showed in the sharpness of his "yes." He came back with one of his own. "Are you?"

"Already have. I got it from the government." Some deep worry shadowed Ryan's eyes. "If a man hasn't got one load, it's another." He seemed tempted to talk about his burden, then shook his head. "The railroad circular bring you out?" At Oakes's nod he said, "Dackett is the man you have to see. He's a hard man to catch." His grin was frosty. "I've been trying for two weeks."

Oakes's eyes were thoughtful. If Ryan had obtained his land from the government, then why did he want to see Dackett? He dismissed the speculation. That was Ryan's business.

"Why can't we buy land outright from the railroad?"

"Because they haven't taken title to it from the government. That keeps them from paying taxes on it. You go damned careful in your dealings with them."

"Is Dackett in there now?"

A bright shine grew in Ryan's eyes. "I think so."

"Then I'll see him."

"I hope you do. He likes to make a man wait.

A man thinks too much while he's waiting, and it blunts his edge. I think I'll stick around to see how you make out."

Oakes nodded and strode into the building.

The office was busy. Four clerks were behind a high counter, and people milled around the section marked "Ticket Office." The clatter of a telegraph key rose above the hum of voices. A man just ahead of Oakes asked for Dackett. He had the mark of the soil on him. His hands were horny and gnarled, and there seemed to be a faint film of dust on him, a patina that even soap and water couldn't remove.

The clerk hardly bothered to look at him. "Did Mr. Dackett send for you?"

The man shook his head.

"Then he's too busy to see you." The clerk's voice sharpened. "You'll be notified when he's ready."

The man muttered an apology and shuffled away. Oakes fumed inwardly. They weren't beggars asking for a handout. They came in here to buy land, and as prospective customers they were entitled to different treatment.

He stepped to the counter and braced his hands on it.

"You!" His voice carried a snap.

The clerk looked up with startled eyes. At least Oakes had his full attention. He also had the attention of everybody else in the room.

"I want to see Dackett. And don't try to tell me he isn't in."

It jarred an affirmative admission out of the clerk, and he nodded before he caught it.

"Then tell him I want to see him. Tell him Oakes Paulson is going to wait out here until he does see me."

The size of the man on the other side of the counter had its effect on the clerk. "I'll tell him. But it won't do you any good."

He stepped to the back of the main office, tapped timidly on a frosted glass door, and waited.

Oakes didn't hear the response, but the clerk opened the door, then shut it behind him. The name on the frosted glass said "Quincy C. Dackett." Oakes settled himself to wait as long as was necessary.

Dackett looked up from his rolltop desk. "What is it, Bryson?"

"A man outside demands to see you, Mr. Dackett."

Dackett's eyes fired. Nobody demanded anything of him. He was a big man in this valley, and he was destined to be even bigger. The valley's commerce passed through his hands. He loaned money, he bought and sold grain. He handled real estate and dealt in mortgages. No one with political ambitions would dare take a step without consulting him. But more important than anything else, he was the representative of the railroad. As such, he knew of and was interested in every consignment of freight. He handled all claims of damage, and it was a rare claimant who was successful against him. He supervised the repair and maintenance of the right-of-way, and no detail of railroad business was too small to escape his attention. Dackett nursed at the udder of the railroad's power and from it grew bigger.

He frowned at the vast map on the wall. It showed the alternate sections owned by the railroad, each section outlined in red. He made a notation on a piece of paper, then looked at Bryson. "Demands, does he? You know what to do with him. And you know better than to come in here bothering me with something like this."

Bryson's eyes were anguished. "I know, Mr. Dackett. But he says he won't leave without seeing you. He's different from the others. I've never seen a bigger, more determined man."

Dackett's eyes picked up interest. "Did you get his name?"

"Oakes Paulson."

Paulson! The wire from Sacramento was still on Dackett's desk. This had to be the same man. Dackett knew from experience that spotting a potential troublemaker early could avoid serious difficulties later. He wanted to see this Paulson; he wanted to beat him down until he was no different than any other man who came into this office.

"Send him in, in a half hour." Enforced waiting was the first club to use. Each passing minute added to its force, beating the belligerence out of a man and letting an insidious worry creep into its place.

He settled back in his chair and watched Bryson leave the office. Too many people were impressed by mere physical bigness. There were other forces besides muscles, and they whipped a man much more thoroughly.

He scowled at a smudge on the cuff of his fine linen shirt. He leaned over and made a note on a pad. These damned clerks would have to learn to clean this office properly. He was proud of his clothes, proud of the money they cost. Poverty was the only inexcusable sin to him. He remembered too many hand-me-downs, too many meals where gruel was about the only food on the table. At the age of fourteen he had broken from his family, and he had never made an attempt to see or learn anything about any of them since. He had come a long way in sixteen years, and he would go a long way further. He was a hungry man, hungry for the things he was building. Wealth and power were the only measurements of a man's ability, and there was no limit to the level to which he could climb. This sunbaked valley wouldn't be all of his world. He knew he was under favorable attention from the San Francisco office. It wasn't inconceivable that he might climb as high as any of the Big Four.

He was surprised when the door opened and Paulson came into the room. The time had passed quickly under his pleasant musings.

Paulson had a belligerence on his face. Apparently the waiting hadn't softened him as Dackett had expected. "Yes?" A lot of men had quailed under that look. Paulson wouldn't be any different.

"I want to know when we get our land." Oakes locked eyes with him. Dackett saw a face chiseled lean, almost to the bone, the jawline prominent, the nose thin and slightly hooked.

Dackett used another club; his position and authority. "I didn't get the name." He purposely mispronounced it after Oakes, and Oakes corrected him. "Paulson. Oakes Paulson."

There seemed to be a quirking to Dackett's lips, as though he was inwardly sneering or laughing. Resentment burned Oakes's face, but before he could speak Dackett picked up a paper from his desk. He studied it until he heard Oakes shift his weight.

"Damn it," Oakes exploded.

Dackett gave him a cold glance. "I'm checking, Mr. Paulson. You haven't even made application for land. And after application is made, you will await your turn. You wouldn't expect to be put ahead of people who were here before you?"

"No, but—"

"You will be notified, Mr. Paulson."

Before he quite knew how it happened Oakes found himself outside the office door. He had an impulse to throw it open, to go back in and make Dackett listen to him. He grinned wryly. Dackett had used logic on him, and Oakes couldn't beat it. He couldn't expect to be put ahead of people here before him. He was bucking a system, a cold, faultless system, and all the fretting and cussing in the world wouldn't put a dent in it.

Ryan saw him coming out of the building and moved to him. "Get anyplace?"

"I saw him. But I hardly got a chance to open my mouth."

Ryan looked disappointed. "I thought you might be the one to break through."

"I wasn't." Ryan's disappointment was an accusing finger. "Did you expect me to pound a special concession out of him?"

"I guess not. Now you'll wait like the rest of them."

"Maybe." Oakes turned his head at the sound of wheels. The bay horse was just stopping before the building. The animal weaved after it halted. The same woman still drove it. If it wasn't already ruined, it was on the edge.

That mocking smile tugged at her lips. Oakes wanted no exchange of words with her; he wanted nothing from her. He nodded to Ryan and crossed the street. Ross was where he had left him, and his eyes were riveted on the woman.

She stood before the horse, looking after Oakes, and a breeze molded her skirt to the full, rich line of her thigh.

Ross whistled, and the sound was a ladle stirring the simmering pot of Oakes's anger. "Does every woman you see mean the same thing to you?"

Ross ignored the question. "Do you know her?"

"No. Come on."

Ross's eyes were suspicious. "Then why is she so interested in you?"

"How the hell do I know? Will you come on?"

Ross caught up with him. "Did you see Dackett?"

"I saw him." Seeing Dackett was no great chore. Getting something out of him was. Despite himself he turned his head. The woman was just going into the railroad building. He speculated briefly upon what she could want in there, and thought sourly, Whatever it is, she'll probably get it.

"Ross, we made a bad mistake coming here. The only thing I'm sure of is that Josie isn't going to spend another night on that siding. We're moving to a hotel."

"But that costs money."

Oakes's eyes were bitter. "It's a little late for

you to be thinking of that. My horse is up the street. It can carry double."

"My horse is at the livery stable." Ross bridled at the searching look Oakes gave him. "A man has to have some way of getting around."

Oakes knew what the horse would be like before he saw it. He wasn't wrong. Ross's mount was a flashy, hot-spirited animal, good for nothing else but riding. Even if it came to an open fight, he was going to make Josie handle Ross's money.

Ross spurred on ahead, whipping up clouds of dust. Riding through it did nothing to help Oakes's temper.

He swung off outside the car on the siding. Josie met him at the doorway. "Ross is sulking about something. He wouldn't even stop." Her eyes searched his face. "It's not good, Oakes?"

"No. We're moving to a hotel, Josie." It would be expensive. But Oakes could see no other course. Something had to change. They couldn't stand many more inroads upon their money, or there wouldn't be much left with which to buy land. His face was gloomy. "We're going to have to watch every penny."

"Ross?"

He gave her a weary nod. "We'll talk about it later." At the moment his indictment of Ross would be too harsh, and he could alienate her. "I'll help you get the stuff ready to move."

He frowned at their pile of belongings in the aisle of the car when Josie called to him from the doorway. It was going to take a wagon to move all this stuff. She called him again, and the odd note in her voice made him look at her.

"Oakes, someone's here to see you."

He walked to the door, and Dackett sat in a buggy. The woman with the taunting eyes was beside him. Oakes saw her look go to Josie, and there was a long weighing in the exchange. Women had a language men would never understand. And it needed no words for them to communicate. A man couldn't understand it, but it always made him uneasy whenever he saw it happening.

Dackett's manner was cordial. He even attempted a stiff smile. "Things are different since we talked, Mr. Paulson. Why didn't you tell me you saved my wife from possibly serious accident?"

Its unexpectedness tied Oakes's tongue in a knot. The woman's eyes grew brighter with some inner amusement.

Dackett nodded. "I'm grateful. I think things can be hastened in your case. Come in and see me in the morning."

He lifted his whip in a salute, tapped the horse with it, and drove off.

Oakes stared after the buggy. She must have learned his name from the clerk, or even from her husband. Why she had told that lie was open to several guesses.

"It looks as though you have a guardian angel," Josie said.

He glanced sharply at her. That had been an odd note in her voice. What was running through her mind; what did she see? He grew uncomfortable under the level directness of her eyes. He could tell her one thing; he didn't want that guardian angel. That one had trouble stamped all over her.

"Let's get busy, Josie. We're still moving into town."

Chapter Six

Oakes regretted that Josie had told Ross of the Dacketts' visit, for Ross insisted upon going in with him in the morning. When Oakes tried to dissuade him, Ross demanded, "It's my land, too, isn't it?"

Oakes couldn't breach that argument, but his face was solemn with thought as they rode toward Dackett's office. Maybe he was crossing a bridge long before the need of one, but he didn't like the Dackett woman having any part in their affairs. Perhaps he made his judgment on too small a knowledge of her, but he had seen enough to be wary. She was strong-willed, and she lacked compassion for horse or man. Those two traits alone were enough to make a man cautious of her, but add her beauty, and Oakes thought a man better be double wary. Dackett had changed directions abruptly. She evidently had influence on him. The why of that influence troubled Oakes.

Ross put it into words. "Dackett switched in a hurry, didn't he?"

Oakes wanted to hear more of Ross's viewpoint. It might help clarify his own. "What do you mean?"

Ross made an impatient gesture. "Yesterday

morning, he wouldn't talk to you. This morning, we're riding in to sign up. What happened in between?"

The same question picked at Oakes. Ross didn't mention the woman, and that was a small relief. Oakes gave her full credit for being the turning point in this. He discarded the idea that it might be because of pity for a family's plight. It didn't fit her, and she certainly wouldn't have had to wait until they came along. There were dozens of families crying for just such help. He came back to the part of the question that scratched him. Could it be because of interest in him? He didn't have a vain bone in his body, and he had snorted when the ridiculous idea first occurred to him. He glanced at Ross. Now, there was a handsome man, and he could believe the woman's interest would reach out to him. Had she made contact with him to get to Ross? He couldn't square that thought, either. That would be giving her credit for too much meticulous planning, for every little detail of their meeting had occurred and flowed with the spontaneity of pure accident. He shook his head. He was giving the matter too much attention, but he didn't like mysteries, particularly when they involved him. He knew he was going to keep his eyes open and examine carefully every offer the Dacketts made. He smiled ruefully. How many times had Josie said he was a suspicious man?

Ross swung down before the rack in front of Dackett's office. He looped his reins and stood for a moment with his arm half draped over his mount's neck. His head was held high as he looked easily up and down the street.

Oakes scowled at the buggy beside Ross's horse. He remembered that buggy. He transferred his scowl to Ross. "Who are you trying to impress?"

Ross's jaw sagged, then a flash of temper appeared in his face. "What the hell are you talking about? You've been in a sour mood all morning." He turned and stamped into the building.

Oakes followed him, a calculating spark in his eyes. Ross's surprise had looked real, but he wasn't accepting it—not totally. He had seen some of Ross's deviousness before.

Bryson didn't attempt to block Oakes this morning. "Mr. Dackett wants to see you the moment you come in." He looked questioningly at Ross before he started for Dackett's door.

Oakes nodded. "My brother." Ross was a surprise to Bryson. Would the same hold with Dackett and his wife?

Bryson opened Dackett's door. Oakes smelled her perfume before he saw her. She sat at one end of Dackett's desk, her face composed. His earlier impressions were only confirmed. She was a disturbingly beautiful woman. She had more directness than most women he knew, for her eyes didn't waver before his.

Ross stared like a damned schoolboy, and Oakes wanted to hit him. He introduced his brother to the Dacketts, and Ross bent overly long above Mrs. Dackett's hand. Oakes tried to read three faces. Ross's thoughts were written openly; the woman's were hidden, and that was no surprise to Oakes. Was that sharpening in Dackett's eyes jealousy? It could readily be, and it would be a normal emotion.

He literally pushed Ross out of the way, and he was aware of two different glances; Ross's angry and resentful, the woman's amused.

Dackett shook Ross's hand with enthusiasm. "Mr. Paulson, I can't tell you how grateful I am to your brother. He saved my wife from severe injury. I woke up in a cold sweat last night thinking about it."

If there was mockery in his face, Oakes couldn't see it. But it could be in the woman's eyes. Ross's mouth was half open, and Oakes was afraid he would push the subject further.

"About our land, Mr. Dackett," he prompted.

"Ah yes, your land. Reta thinks you should have the best available in the valley, and I'm in agreement with her. There is a piece open near some acres we own, and I can assure you it is fine ground. I've had the papers made out. Just as soon as you sign, you can move onto your new land."

Oakes shook his head. He guessed he was grateful for their help, but it sounded as though he was being rushed into something. "I'd like to sort of look around a little first, Mr. Dackett."

He saw the angry red tinge creeping up Dackett's neck. Ross looked as though he was about to protest, and Oakes put a hard look on him. It surprised him to see only amusement on Reta's face.

She checked Dackett's growing anger. "Quincy, I don't think that's unreasonable. Mr. Paulson should look around. He's picking out his home."

Ross's jaw jutted. "I'm picking out my home, too. And I say anything that Mr. Dackett selects will be fine with me."

Oakes took a harsh breath, but before he could speak Dackett shook his head. "No, your brother is right, Mr. Paulson. In my eagerness to help I overlooked one thing. A man has to see his land, hold it in his hands, before he knows this is the ground for him. I forgot that. You take your time and look around. When you find what you want, you come back."

This was as open and straightforward as Oakes could want. His face cleared. "Fine, fine. We'll be back in a few days."

He took Ross's elbow and pushed him toward the door. He didn't want Ross opening his mouth. He turned his head and nodded to the Dacketts before he drew the door after him.

• • •

Dackett's lip curled as he looked at his wife. "That didn't work out the way you expected, did it?"

She gave him that maddening slow smile. "Did I expect it to work out a certain way, Quincy?"

She could infuriate him quicker than any person he knew. It was hard to believe that he had once thought himself in love with her. She had tricked him into that belief, and he would never forgive her for that. In one of their frequent quarrels she had admitted she never loved him. She had picked him because she had seen he was on his way upward, and she had wanted him to carry her along on that climb. Her submissiveness was the only thing she gave him, and it was worthless to him.

He sat there staring at her, and all the old thoughts were again in his mind. But they no longer had the power to rake him. He had tried his best to break her, but she had a will of iron. Now they went their separate ways, and each was useful to the other. For each filled out the picture that society demanded. She was a beautiful wife, and she ran a gracious house. He furnished the necessaries for her to live as she wished. He knew many a man envied him, and he suspected it would be a rare woman in this town who wouldn't have traded places with her.

At his unconscious smile her eyes sharpened. "What amuses you, Quincy?"

"I was just thinking of how much envy this town wastes on the two of us." He made a ritual of lighting a cigar. "I have been wondering how long it would be before your eye would stray again."

Her quickened breathing made her words jerky. "What do you mean by that?"

"You don't think I believed that runaway story, did you? Haven't I seen you handle horses? What impressed you about him? His size?"

He delighted in the white, pinched look around her lips, in the faint rush of color into her face. Rarely did he shatter her composure. "If I hadn't suggested that letting him get his land as soon as he could might be an excellent method of repaying him, would you have thought of it, my dear?" He blew out a smoke ring and laughed. "When you agreed so eagerly, it only confirmed what I thought. I never saw you show any interest in the emigrant families before."

He watched her struggle to regain her scattered thoughts. "You're wondering why I did it," he went on. "Perhaps his size impressed me, too." His eyes glinted wickedly. "Though not in the same manner it did you. I thought a great deal about him after he left my office yesterday. He's the kind of man who attracts others to him. And powerful enough to awe them. He raises a tempest wherever he goes. First at Sacramento, and here with Wiley and Henshaw. They won't be the last. I think I'd rather have that kind with me than against me. Sometimes a small favor can tie them to you. And you gave me the excuse to offer it."

He laughed until tears filled his eyes. "Don't look so angry, my dear. It works for your benefit, too. I say nothing about how you spend your time, and he is grateful to both of us."

He stood suddenly and crossed to her. He seized her wrist, and the way she winced showed how deeply his fingers bit. "But I want to know everything he does. And don't try to outsmart me, Reta. There's unrest in this valley, all directed at me. If they ever get strong enough to overthrow me, you'd go, too. Your house, your clothes, your horses. Don't ever lose sight of that."

He let go of her wrist. "It isn't working out too badly, Reta. We're both getting the things that are important to us."

She didn't say a word, and he smiled. "I thought you'd see it that way."

Chapter Seven

Outside Dackett's office, Ross poked Oakes in the ribs. "No wonder you didn't want me cutting in."

Oakes fixed him with hard eyes. "Was that in your mind?"

Ross colored. "You know what I mean. I guess rescuing her gives you a prior claim."

"I don't know what you mean. And I've got no claim of any kind."

Ross blinked. "But I heard Dackett say—"

"And I can't help what Dackett says."

Ross looked dismayed. "You're not going to turn down his offer?"

"I'll sign up just as fast as I can—if I'm satisfied. But we're going to look around first."

"You'll end up by offending him. Did you see his face, when you refused to sign now?"

"How would you handle it, Ross?"

"The least you can do is to look at that land."

"I don't have to look at it first." Oakes looked across the street and yelled, "Ryan. Hold up a minute."

"What do you want him for?"

"I'm going to ask him to show us around."

"I'll be damned if I can figure how you think. You turn down Dackett who can help us, and pick up Ryan who, who—" He hunted for the right expression.

"Who can't do anything for us," Oakes finished.

"Well, can he?"

Oakes grinned. "I don't know. I haven't known him long enough." He started toward Ryan. "Ross, stay away from the Dacketts. I don't want you asking either of them to show you that land."

He caught the shiftiness in Ross's eyes. It had been on his mind. "I mean it, Ross." Ryan was almost to them. "Drop it."

Ryan's eyes flicked from face to face. Ross hardly offered a civil greeting. If it bothered Ryan, it didn't show.

"What can I do for you, Oakes?"

"Are you willing to let me impose on you?"

"For anything but money."

Oakes returned Ryan's grin. He would say this man would wear well. "I'd like to see some land. Will you show me around?"

"Sure. But it might not do you any good. Lately the railroad has been shoving a piece of land at a man and saying take it or leave it. After all his waiting, he usually takes it."

"I'd just like to look around."

"I didn't think I'd change your mind." Ryan put an oblique glance on Ross. "You coming?"

"No." The word was said with unusual violence, but it didn't put a flicker in Ryan's face.

Oakes let his anger show. "Then go back and stay with Josie. She's been left alone too much lately."

Ross's wild look broke against Oakes's eyes. He whirled without a word, and his stride was long and furious.

Ryan didn't look as though he expected an explanation, but Oakes felt as though one was due him. "I apologize for his manners. He's mad at me, and he's taking it out on you. It seems every time you see us we're arguing."

Ryan's eyes twinkled. "If I was mad at you, I'd take it out on somebody else, too. A younger brother can be headstrong."

My God, Oakes thought. I'm two years younger, and I look older. Maybe accepting responsibilities ages a man too fast.

Ryan pointed across the street. "A friend of yours just ducked back inside the door. Wiley."

Oakes grinned, and now the seriousness was on Ryan's face. "Don't make the mistake of discounting him. When his hand heals, he'll try to put a more soothing salve on it than any the doctor used. Your hide."

Oakes shrugged. "He's got to skin it first."

Ryan half laughed. "And that could be interesting. My horse is around the corner. I'll meet you back here."

When Ryan came back he asked, "Anything in particular you want to see?"

"Is there any government land left?"

"If there is, it's rocky and ditched. The railroad holds the rest, and nobody knows where anything stands. Some say the Southern Pacific didn't properly fulfill their contract, and all the land through here is forfeited by them and goes back to public domain. The Secretary of the Interior has ordered the railroad privileges revoked on twenty alternate sections of land. But the railroad has power of its own. It's thrown the Secretary's order into court, and most everybody is betting the courts will decide in favor of the railroad. So far, every decision has been decided that way."

"Then I might as well forget government land."

"Around here, yes. And you won't know what your railroad land will cost you. A preemption claim of a hundred and sixty acres with the government would have cost you a dollar and a quarter an acre. Or you could have picked up eighty acres free by living on it for three years."

"But the railroad's circular said—"

Ryan snorted. "I've seen them, but I don't believe them. I tell you that damned railroad will gouge. They do on everything they touch. They keep raising their freight rates when they haven't got a reason. They'll find a way to do the same with their land. I wouldn't trust them as far as I can throw one of their engines."

Galen Mundro had said about the same thing. Oakes had heard a lot of words about the Southern Pacific. He couldn't remember a favorable one.

"Then which way does a man turn?"

Ryan blew out his lips. "He can wait for a court decision and hope the land goes back to the government. But the decision might not be favorable, and his waiting would be lost. Or he can go ahead and take up railroad land and hope this time they play fair."

"What's your opinion?"

"Damn it, Oakes. I wouldn't know. If the settlers stand together against the railroad, they might be able to back them up. But will they stand together? I don't know. Still want to look at land?"

Oakes's smile was strained at the edges. "I've come a long way and spent some money. At least I ought to get to look at some land for it."

Ryan headed out of town. "I thought you would. There's a piece of land I'd like you to see first. I think it lays mighty sweet."

They rode mostly in silence, Ryan breaking it every now and then to point out something of interest. Then he started talking in a steady stream. "Lots of wheat raised around here, though it's beginning to slip. This land will produce too much to tie it up in a single crop a year. That dried grass you see on the hills is wild oats. Dries up early in the summer. It's good cattle feed, but a man can do better with other things than cattle. Yes, the summers are always dry. The rains come from October to March. My God, you'll think some of them are going to wash you away. That line of trees? Eucalyptus. Imported from Australia for firewood. Grows like a weed. Especially the second growth. That's live oak over there. Stays green the year around. It isn't like the oak you know. The wood's on the punky side."

Oakes's part of the talk was an occasional nod. He couldn't have picked a better guide.

Ryan stopped at the top of a rise, and his manner was casual. "I think this is a pretty little valley."

It was. What wasn't flat was gently rolling, no bar to horse or plow. And clearing wasn't going to be a great problem, for trees and brush were sparse. They grew thicker below them and to the left, and Oakes's eyes gleamed. Usually a clump of trees like that indicated a spring, or water of some kind. He couldn't be sure without going closer, but some of those trees looked like willow.

"That a spring down there?"

Ryan grinned. "I saw you spot it. It's a wet-weather spring. Surface water in the rainy season. But the trees around it stay green all year. Be a nice spot to build close to."

"Ah," Oakes murmured. This was the land Ryan had wanted him to see all the time. He studied it with new interest.

Ryan respected his silence for some time. "It has quite a few advantages. The irrigation ditches will come in from over there." He pointed toward the northwest. "A long reach of them is already dug. This piece of land will get water about as soon as any in the valley. And you'd be starting out with a pretty good neighbor."

"Who?"

Ryan chuckled. "Me. I own the land next to this. The next section was government land. I tell you I debated a long time before I decided against this place. You know what swung me." He paused. "We're into nice weather. A man could live in a tent without any inconvenience at all."

A smile tugged at Oakes's lips. "You wouldn't just happen to have a tent, would you?"

Ryan frowned thoughtfully. "By God, I just remembered I do." He grinned sheepishly at Oakes's laugh. "All right, I tried to be sneaky and get you here. But a good neighbor is about as important a thing as a man can have. If you can get this land from the railroad, I've got a wagon to move your stuff out here. And I'm a fair hand when it comes to throwing up a house."

He was making it more attractive by the minute. "You're not trying to influence me, are you, Ryan?"

Ryan looked shocked. "The idea didn't enter my head."

"I didn't think it had. I'm still going to look at other land."

Ryan's face sobered. "I knew you would, Oakes."

Oakes spent four more days looking, but he was ruined from the start, and he knew it. The land Ryan had showed him kept getting in his way and blocking his vision. Maybe he was foolish in not looking at the land Dackett had proposed, but he didn't like the thought of being too close to the man.

He had asked Ryan an offhand question about Dackett's land, and Ryan had said, "Which piece do you mean? He owns several of them. The man's a hog. No trough can hold enough to satisfy him." Ryan's eyes had turned bleak. "Never get under obligation to him."

Oakes nodded. That was about the way he had it figured.

Ryan tried to disguise the anxiety in his face. "Have you decided on your land yet?"

"Just about." Oakes guessed he had really decided from the moment he saw it. He had to bring Ross out and get his approval. What if Ross didn't like it? Then it was just going to be too bad, for this was one time Ross wasn't going to have a hell of a lot to say about it. He hadn't earned it; he hadn't spent a minute of time looking.

Ryan sighed. "I was going to hold it as a club over your head and not offer my wagon to any other piece of land. But I'll move you anyplace you want to go."

Oakes threw back his head and laughed. "I kind of thought you would." No, he wouldn't tell Ryan this afternoon. He wouldn't tell him until the direction of the wagon made it impossible to keep it hidden any longer.

Chapter Eight

Oakes stopped his work as he listened to Josie's singing. An unconscious smile was on his face. It had been a long time since she had been in that kind of mood. A tent didn't make much of a home, but she was content with it for the present. And Ross wasn't causing either of them any trouble. Maybe it was only the newness holding him, but for now, he seemed willing and interested. He was out there somewhere struggling with some stubborn brush.

It took a lot of effort and time just to keep up with the survival chores. They could get water from Ryan's place, but it had to be hauled. He had borrowed Ryan's wagon more than he should. He was going to have to pick up one as soon as he could.

Oakes frowned as he resumed work. There were so many things to buy and so much to do that if a man dwelt on them, he could drive himself crazy. He had eliminated the immediate need of a pole corral by hobbling the horses. That way the horses could feed themselves. The problem of watering them remained. When a man had to haul water to horses, he watched every drop they drank with a jaundiced eye. They needed a garden, too, but he would be damned before he hauled water to a garden.

To an impatient man it looked as though they were crawling, but if he stopped and took careful inventory, he could see a small progress. He had managed to give a couple of afternoons to the digging of the irrigation ditches, and that work fascinated him. He only wished he had solid stretches of time to give to it. When those ditches were dug and running full was when the real progress started. The fresnos cut easily through the sandy soil. Looking at the raw, fresh scar of the ditch behind them, a man still found it hard to believe that anything would grow in this sere country. But it would, and water was the lifegiving force. Next, a man found it hard to believe there was even water in this same world. But other men told him it was there in the distant purple shadows of the mountains, ample, cool, tumbling water, which—once the ditches were dug—would deliver itself here through the force of gravity. Too many of them said the same thing for it not to be believable. Whenever the heat got too rough, a man could stop and wipe his face while he glanced at those distant mountains. He wasn't actually cooler as he thought of that cool, tumbling water, but it helped.

Oakes looked at the dropping sun and shook his head. This day was about finished, for there wasn't much twilight out here. It was a strange country in many ways, but it had a way of fastening its hold on a man. He thought living would be more than acceptable out here, if he could just catch up to the point where he could slow down to a fast trot. He wanted to put in more time on those ditches, and he wanted to start a house and try and dig a well. He had a feeling that the wet-water spring Ryan had pointed out the first time he had seen this land could be deepened into something interesting. Ryan had agreed and had said, "Let me know when you're ready to start." But damn it, Ryan had done enough as it was. He couldn't keep on calling on him forever. What he needed was four times the normal number of hours in a day and a dozen more pairs of hands—and no need of sleep. Then he just might possibly begin to catch up a little.

They had erected two tents, one that Ryan loaned them, and the smaller one Oakes had bought in town. Living in a tent in this climate wasn't rough, and he didn't mind it, but it had to be different with Josie. No matter how much she tried she couldn't turn a tent into a home. Her fight with the dust and sand was a never-ending thing. He sympathized with her with all his heart, but he couldn't change his decision. The need for an available water supply was the greatest pinch right now; the well had to come first. He was going to hate to see her face when he announced it. He attacked his work more savagely. He would have to tell her tonight. He wanted to start the well in the morning.

At supper Ross announced, "I got that patch of brush cleared out, Oakes. We're getting closer to plowing."

"Good." Oakes couldn't look at Josie. The eagerness in her eyes would kill him. How well he remembered her words. "I know how long it takes to build a house, Oakes. I'm not asking for all of it now. All I'm asking for is a floor. Just something to raise us up out of the dust and sand. I won't mind canvas walls and roof for a while longer."

What a liar he was. For he had said heartily, "That's our next project, Josie."

Putting off telling her was only going to make it worse. He was right about that eagerness in her face; it was so visible that it shone. Now he had to step on that eagerness, and it was a form of killing.

"Josie." He gulped and steadied his voice. "We've got to start the well in the morning."

It knocked the light out of her eyes. He had to make her understand. "Josie, listen to me. We can't go on hauling water from Ryan's. A well will ease your work, and it'll sure help Ross and me. Just as soon as the well is dug . . ." His voice trailed away.

He wished those eyes wouldn't stare so directly at him. He had to make her another promise, but it was swelling in his mouth so much he couldn't get it out.

"Josie, I promise—"

She jumped to her feet, and a momentary wildness was in her eyes. "Don't you think I'm trying to be patient. Don't you think—" She made a tremendous effort to regain control of herself. "It's so hot in here. I'm going outside for a little while."

Ross watched her push through the flaps. "What's bothering her tonight?"

"Heat, work, monotony. And her tomorrows look too much like today."

Ross's face twisted in quick anger. "Why, damn it. Doesn't she think we know the same thing?"

Oakes looked at him in disgust. All Josie needed was for Ross to put his arms about her and tell her that tomorrow would be better. A woman could be satisfied with a mighty little promise, if the right man said it. "It's different with a woman, Ross."

"Like hell it is."

The hot words crowded into Oakes's mouth, but he held them. They were all strained and edgy tonight. "Simmer down, boy."

"Who does she think I'm doing all this work for? Doesn't she appreciate—"

Oakes glared at him. Ross had a longer memory than this, and Oakes wasn't going to let him get away with it. "We had all this kind of work done back in Ohio. She had a house there."

Ross's eyes rolled. It reminded Oakes a little

of a horse that was thinking about breaking. And maybe that was what Ross was working up to. Routine galled Ross's shoulders, and he couldn't stand too much of it. He threw up his hands as he said, "I guess I'll be blamed for everything that goes wrong out here. Because I suggested a move I thought would be good for us."

"Oh, hell, Ross." Oakes stopped in helplessness. Ross said "suggested." He had done everything he could to force the move.

"I haven't been off this goddamned place since I saw it. But that doesn't mean anything to you two. Josie accuses me with big, sorrowful eyes, and you're always criticizing me."

They were close to another big, open quarrel, and Oakes wanted to plunge into it as eagerly as Ross. But it wouldn't change a thing. This wasn't the answer. It only made it worse.

He stood and made a slashing gesture with the edge of his palm. "Drop it, Ross."

Ross still hollered; he probably got a special release out of it, and he was making good progress on Oakes's faults.

Oakes turned at the tent entrance. "Ross, we've got to live together. Until both of us are ready to do something about that, this isn't doing us any good." He parted the flaps and stepped outside.

Sure, he was breathing hard. He felt anger as readily as the next one; he was no saint. In the morning he and Ross wouldn't quite meet each other's eyes, and there wouldn't be more than a word or two. They'd add a few words every so often, and by afternoon they would be talking again because that was what they both wanted. But it was a hell of a way to end a quarrel.

He saw Josie's silhouette just beyond the big live oak tree and moved to her. "Josie, I'm sorry."

For a moment he was afraid she wasn't going to answer him; then her words, almost indistinct, drifted to him. "For what?"

"For lying to you."

"Oh, Oakes, you didn't." Tears in a voice could make it sound shaky like that.

"No difference. I made you a promise I couldn't keep, and maybe I knew I couldn't at the time."

Laughter had the upper hand now. "I know the well is more important, Oakes. And sand is softer to walk on than a wooden floor. I just don't know when I'm well off."

Soberly, he stared at her. "You're quite a gal, Josie. I upset everybody tonight. Ross is mad at me."

He saw the familiar softness come into her face. "Poor Ross. He has been working hard."

He felt the old prickle of resentment. Other men worked hard and didn't expect anything to be made out of it. But Ross got special credit of it. "Don't let him sit alone, Josie."

She missed the edge in his voice, for she smiled at him and turned toward the tent, her own need forgotten. He watched her enter and saw the figures silhouetted on the tent walls. The figures merged, and the old loneliness returned with more force than ever.

He sighed and moved toward his own tent. He lighted the lamp and pulled off his shirt. The lamp globe shattered into a million bits, and he was frozen with the shock of it. The report of the rifle came instantly after, sounding not too far away. It was followed by another, coming before he could dive from his feet.

He hit the ground hard and tried to flatten himself under the cot. The interior of the tent seemed to be filled with buzzing, angry insects, and the tent walls were becoming pocked with holes. Some of the bullets made two holes, and he imagined he could hear the ripping tears as they passed through the tent. He certainly heard the more solid whacks the slugs made hitting something denser than a tent wall; that metallic clang over there had to be a wash basin or a bucket. He heard bullets smash into boxes and supplies he had stacked outside, and he thought he understood what the marksman was after. Whoever it was was trying to shoot hell out of everything they owned, and he wasn't wasting a lot of time in worrying about somebody getting nicked.

A man can only be frightened so far, then he runs out of room on that road and has to go back the other way until he finally winds up in anger. Oakes crawled to the entrance and listened. There were two of them out there. The volume and direction of the fire told him so, and they were making sieves out of both of the tents. The wink of flame from the base of a tree told him where one of them was, and his rage grew. He could put his hands on an ax, but what was he going to do with it—throw it? He had an old horse pistol packed away somewhere, but right now he couldn't say where. The pistol and the ax were in the same worthless class. Those two riflemen were having themselves a hell of a time, and Oakes would have given about anything he owned to get his hands on them for just a few seconds.

The other tent was catching its share of punishment, and fear for Josie and Ross was a hard knot in his throat. He might be able to dash across the short intervening distance and reach them, but what good could he do there? About the only thing he could accomplish would be to overcrowd the tent.

"Ross. Josie. Are you all right?"

Ross's voice answered. "Oakes, who are they? What do they want? What are we going to do?"

Oakes could answer only one of the questions. "Stay on the ground. Is Josie all right?"

"I'm all right, Oakes." Her voice certainly wasn't any more strained than Ross's.

Oakes discarded a dozen ideas, each getting a little more impractical. He couldn't see a damned thing they could do. About all that was left was to wait until the riflemen tired of their sport or ran out of ammunition, and if one or the other didn't happen soon, he was going to choke on his own fury.

He heard a heavier, deeper boom, and that could only be made by a shotgun. It was followed by a startled yell, and a savage voice shouted, "Come on, you bastards." The night was blasted again by that heavy, full-throated report.

A figure jumped to its feet and ran in a twisting, ducking course. Oakes couldn't name it; he never got a clear view of it at any time. He didn't see the other one, but he heard the slam of running steps.

He hadn't heard much of that new voice, but he thought he recognized it. "Ryan?" he called hopefully, and stepped out of the tent.

"Oakes? Any of you hurt?" A dark figure hurried toward him, and Oakes saw the shotgun it carried in its left hand.

"Ryan!" He put the rest of his relief into the hard handclasp he gave him.

"What the hell was going on, Oakes?"

"It doesn't make sense. It looks as though all they wanted was to put a few holes through everything we own. Did you get a look at them?"

Ryan shook his head. "I couldn't get that close. A shotgun doesn't argue on equal terms with a rifle. I was hoping they'd run. I figure myself lucky they did."

Ross and Josie were coming toward them.

Josie nodded in response to Oakes's searching look. "I'm all right. Who were they, Oakes? And why?"

"I don't know. They shot up things pretty good. And it wouldn't have ended, if Ryan hadn't come along." He put a puzzled look on Ryan. "How did you happen along at just this time?"

"I've got some shovels in the back of the wagon I thought you might need in the morning. I wasn't busy tonight. I thought I'd bring them over."

"Look at what they did," Josie wailed, and flew into the damage.

Oakes pulled Ryan to one side. If he had to make a guess, he would say Ryan was probably lonesome tonight. But he was grateful to whatever reason had brought him over here. "Do you always carry a shotgun in the wagon?"

Ryan looked sheepish. "I do ever since that damned wolf killed my dog. I keep hoping I'll get a snap shot at him. I heard the firing quite a way off and came the rest of the way on foot, hoping to sneak up on them. Wish I could have seen who they were for you, Oakes."

"I think I know."

Ryan's eyes widened, and Oakes nodded. "I haven't been here long enough to make very many enemies. Dackett wouldn't get this mad at me because I turned down land he picked out for me, would he?"

"Wiley?"

"Has to be. Who'd get any gain out of this kind of damage except a man with a hate? Can I take your wagon?"

Ryan eyed him shrewdly. "You figuring on going to town tonight?"

"I am."

"But you don't know it was Wiley. Do you even have a gun?"

"I can take a look at his face and know. And I've got your shotgun."

"Then we're wasting time talking." Ryan laughed as Oakes blinked. "You don't think I'm going to let you go in alone, do you?"

Oakes studied Ryan's determined face. "All right. But you stay out of it after we get there."

Neither of them talked much on the way in. At the outskirts of town Oakes asked, "Ryan, can I come borrowing again? Can I take your wagon in the morning?"

"You know you can."

"I'd like to get a load of lumber. I promised Josie I'd build her a platform for her tent. I guess nothing makes a woman happier than getting her feet out of the dust."

"I thought you were hurting to get that well started."

"I am. But it can wait a little longer." After tonight, Josie's floor came before anything else.

Ryan stopped before the saloon where Wiley ran his game. "Oakes, what are you going to say to him?"

"I'm going to look. And let him start the saying."

Ryan nodded. It could be effective. He would hate to have a guilty conscience and have this big man staring at him.

Wiley wasn't running his usual game. Oakes asked one of the players where he was, and the man shrugged. "Haven't seen him all evening. He said earlier he was going over to Henshaw's office."

Oakes turned and tramped outside. He headed for Henshaw's office, and Ryan fell into step with him. "Ryan, does Wiley strike you as the kind of a man who'd keep anybody posted on where he was going?"

"Not unless he had a definite reason for it."

"That's kind of my figuring on it, too."

They stepped into Henshaw's office, and Wiley sat at one end of the desk. He turned his head toward them, and Oakes couldn't tell whether or not there was an unusual alertness in the gesture.

Oakes just stood there, staring, and Henshaw

fidgeted first. "What's the hell eating you? Damn it, if you've got a reason for coming in here, say it."

"Somebody shot hell out of my place a little while ago."

Henshaw's face tightened. "Can you name him?"

"I wouldn't be surprised." Oakes resumed staring at Wiley.

Color crept up from Henshaw's collar. "Goddamn it. Then name him, and quit pussyfooting around."

"I guess it wouldn't do any good to ask Wiley where he was this evening."

"So that's what's gnawing you. You couldn't be farther wrong. He's been right here all evening. We've just been sitting here jawing."

Oakes swung his eyes to Ryan. "What do you think?"

"I think we got some of the biggest liars in the world right here in this county."

Henshaw's face burned bright. "Lookit here, Ryan."

Oakes leaned forward. "Don't you want to be called a liar, Sheriff? I'll make Ryan take it back, if I can look at Wiley's horse and rifle."

Did a nerve in Wiley's cheek jump? Oakes wasn't sure. But his proposal certainly increased Henshaw's bluster.

"I told you where he was. I don't have to prove

my word to you at any time. Now, get out of here."

"Sure I've got my answer." Oakes stabbed a finger at Wiley. "Let me tell you something. What happened tonight better hadn't happen again. If I get any more damage of any kind, I'm asking for no help from Henshaw. I'm coming straight for you, and nobody's going to get in between us."

Wiley stared at the floor, and what could be seen of his face was twisted and bitter.

Oakes grinned at Ryan when he got outside. "What do you think?"

"It might tie him down. Henshaw's a nervous man, and he doesn't like trouble. He may put a hobble on Wiley, too." His laugh was a short burst of harsh amusement. "Wiley's face didn't leave much room for doubt, did it?"

Oakes lengthened his stride. "None, I'd say."

Dackett leaned forward in his chair, and his voice snapped when he spoke. "Don't look at me like that, Wiley. I told Henshaw to send you to me. And don't blame him. It's his job to keep order. You ought to be grateful to him. He saved your ass for you last night."

Wiley's eyes smoldered. "Do you think I'm afraid of Paulson?"

"If you had any sense, you would be." Dackett shook his head in disgust. "I never could understand how a man like you thinks. What did you accomplish? I mean really accomplish. You tore up things, and it didn't put a dime in your pocket or set you a step nearer any goal you wanted. You go ahead and suck on your satisfaction, and see how long the sweet taste lasts." He leaned back and weighed Wiley. "Paulson wasn't playing around with you. Take another step against him, and it could be your last."

"I'll blow his goddamned head off for him."

Dackett's face flamed with quick fury. "You idiot. The one thing I've been fighting to avoid. You shoot Paulson, and every damned farmer in the valley will pick up his fight. And him being dead won't stop it." He composed his face. "You know, Wiley, the easiest way out of this is maybe for me to throw you to the wolves."

He grinned sardonically at Wiley's display of fear. Wiley knew how much he needed Dackett's backing to keep on operating. If Dackett stepped from under him, Wiley was through.

"Quincy, it won't happen again."

"I didn't think it would, Wiley. Stay in line, and I may let you have him one of these days."

He liked the confusion in Wiley's face. First Dackett protected Paulson, then he talked of getting rid of him. Wiley could never understand that timing made the position a man took on anything.

"He's a powerful man physically, Wiley. And it will carry some influence. I'd rather have him with me, and I may be able to hold him. But that rope could break, Wiley. Then it might not be worthwhile trying to find one that will hold him. It might be simpler to just get rid of him. How'd you like for me to save that job for you?"

Wiley didn't answer. The gleam in his eyes did it for him.

Chapter Nine

The flooring for the tent took time and work, and Oakes regretted the time more than the work. It took time to assemble all the materials, work and time to level the ground before he could actually begin building. The sawing and nailing consumed more of his basic two ingredients, and it took more time to move everything out of the tent onto the finished floor and reerect the tent over it. He was grumbling about the day being shot to hell when Josie came over and looked at her new floor. She stared at it a long time without saying a word, then she turned her head toward him. The shine in her eyes was enough. It quite wiped out any regret he had for the lost day.

He had recognized the growing restlessness in Ross and had given him the day off. He could handle the floor by himself, but Ross had better be here in the morning, for Oakes was going to start that well come hell or high water. And that wasn't a one-man job.

He was still awake when Ross rode in that night. It was a respectable hour, and Oakes nodded in satisfaction. Maybe this move had been a good thing after all. Ross was either growing up or gaining a sense of responsibility. He chuckled as he thought about it. Weren't the two the same thing?

He started the well early in the morning, and the digging was easy. Too easy. He would have preferred a little clay mixed with that sand. This could take a lot more work than he had expected, for if the well had to go deep at all, the walls would have to be shored and rocked; shored as he went down, rocked after the digging was finished. He scowled at the shifting soil. If he needed shoring, it meant borrowing Ryan's wagon for a trip to town after lumber. Ryan was going to be sick of the sight of him. He made himself a vow. He would buy a wagon at the earliest opportunity.

Ross hadn't said a word for an hour, and his face had a peculiar tightness. Oakes thought in irritation, Did he have that much to drink last night? Then an old scene that he had thought was no longer in his head, hit him. As kids, they had dug a cave in back of the barn in Ohio. And that cave had tumbled in, burying Ross. Oakes had dug frantically with his bare hands, clearing Ross's head, and Ross was alive when he reached him. No real harm had been done, but he remembered the nightmares Ross had had for a long time after that. Was that old memory riding Ross now? His face looked like it. He wanted to ask Ross about it, but Ross would hotly deny it. Oakes could appreciate an old, deeply buried fear gripping a man with a hold he couldn't break. He would keep Ross on top. That wouldn't erase the fears, but it should ease them.

He was down better than six feet by now, and he had fought minor cave-ins all the way. It meant much more digging, for the hole had to be made bigger than needed, especially at the top. It would have been smarter to have stopped and gotten his shoring lumber, but he thought the sand was getting a little damper, and he wanted to see what the next shovelful did. Wouldn't it be something if he could bring in a well at this shallow depth?

He could still throw the dirt out of the hole, but it took a long heave, and the effort was demanding. It wouldn't be long before he had to put up a windlass.

He hit hardpan, and the going slowed to a crawl. He wouldn't have to do much shoring in this stuff. It should stand as well as a rock wall. It was far harder than clay, and it had to be picked out a chunk at a time. Then he had to throw the broken-out chunks out of the hole.

He attacked that hardpan with all his strength, and each blow of the pick sent little streams of sand cascading down around him. He was making more work for himself, for the sand meant additional shoveling, but he was impatient to break through the hardpan. He could be lucky enough to find sheet water under it.

He drove in the point of the pick with all his might. He felt a shudder run through the earth, and at first thought he had cracked the hardpan.

Then he felt a shifting all around him, a sort of gentle collapsing. He was still bent from his last blow, the point of the pick buried, and he looked up in alarm. The walls were falling down on him.

"Ross!" His voice was pitched high. "Ross!"

It seemed as though everything moved in slow motion, but in reality it moved fast. He was already buried to his thighs, and still the sand poured down. He tried to kick through it, and the weight pinioned his legs. He let go of the pick and flailed at the sand with his hands, and in a tick of time, it was higher than his waist.

"Ross!" Now there was a shrillness in his voice.

Ross peered down at him, a white, frightened face with the power to reason erased from it.

"Ross!" Oakes felt as though he were ripping his lungs out in the effort to strike through that blind fear on Ross's face. If that crazy white fear held in Ross's face, it wouldn't take much to make him bolt.

The sand was almost up to his shoulders, and he heard the sob break in Ross's throat. Then the face was gone. He yelled until his throat was raw, but he knew that face wasn't coming back. He had two hopes now, both of them faint: that Josie would hear him, or that the sand would stop. It seemed that he had lived a lifetime in terror, but it couldn't have been more than split seconds, for he hadn't fully straightened. And that was going to hurt him, for it put his head lower in the hole.

He yelled as the sand touched his chin, a harsh, tearing animal bleat of terror, with no particular name or thought behind it. Then his mouth was covered, and he drew a deep breath and shut his eyes. He had a few seconds left at best, and he couldn't use them. He exerted all his strength, and he couldn't move a muscle. Panic ran its clammy fingers down his spine, and if his mouth hadn't been blocked, he would have been screaming and raving. This wasn't the way it should end, entrapped in this dead-heavy weight that left a man helpless and terrified.

His lungs were bursting with the effort of holding his breath, and a swimming red haze had penetrated his closed lids. Suddenly he felt greater weight in the area above his head, and thought that a great chunk of a wall must have let go. But this weight had movement; he could feel it stirring around above him. Then something was scooping sand away from his face.

He breathed in sand with his first gasping breath and unwisely opened his mouth before the sand was cleared away. He took in more sand, making his tongue feel heavy and gritty.

But those were petty discomforts. He could breathe, and those frantic hands cleared more sand from his face with every scoop.

He thought it was Ross rescuing him. Then his eyes cleared, and he saw Ryan's harried face.

He spit out sand until his tongue was free, and

he babbled worse than an old woman, but after a man had lived an eternity of hell as he had, he was entitled to babble.

Ryan's frantic digging slowed, and Oakes saw that his nails were bleeding. "Are you all right?" Ryan asked, and at Oakes's nod he exploded. "You damned fool! Digging in this stuff by yourself. You're going to have to shore up every foot of it."

"I found that out. I wasn't by myself. Ross was—" Oakes stopped abruptly. He hadn't meant to say that.

Ryan stared bleakly at him. "Did he run out on you?"

He had to take the harsh judging out of Ryan's eyes. "He went for help, Ryan."

Ryan scooped a violent handful of sand from Oakes's shoulder. "Shit! You'd have been dead before he could even think of getting back."

Oakes didn't want that cold contempt for Ross, and he searched for words to erase it. He told Ryan about the cave-in Ross had been trapped in as a child, of the terror that had taken so long to ease.

Ryan's face didn't soften. "That was a long time ago. How long's a man going to milk an incident like that?"

Oakes sighed. He hadn't been able to make Ryan understand at all.

Ryan went on, "Oakes, this is going to make

you sore, because he's your brother. Don't ever rely on him too much. Because he'll slide out from under you just when you need him most." He turned his head and dug steadily. "You can't see it, or you won't see it. You try to do most of his walking for him. I guess you've done it so long you can't break the habit."

"Goddamn it. It's none of your business."

"You're right." Ryan looked over his shoulder. "He's coming with Josie."

Oakes heard the pound of running feet. This talk would have to be postponed, but he wasn't through with it yet. He was in debt to Ryan for a lot of things, but certainly not enough to let him say anything he wanted about Oakes's family.

Josie's face was a mask of terror. Ross wouldn't look at him.

Ryan bobbed his head at her in sympathy. "Josie, he's all right."

She gulped for a mouthful of air, and the fear lost its hold on her face.

Ryan had a brutal weighing in his eyes. "Ross, help me get him out."

Ross didn't want to get down into that hole, and it showed.

Ryan's lip curled. "It's caved all it's going to. You're safe."

Ross couldn't meet anybody's eyes. Oakes had never seen a sicker look on a man's face. And a suffering was in Josie's eyes, too. He opened his mouth to jump all over Ryan, then slowly closed it. He couldn't say anything, not with her here. Ross had a particular kind of hell to live with. But the sorry part was he couldn't keep it to himself; he had to distribute it around to the people who loved him.

Ross tried to meet Ryan's eyes. "I thought going for help was the most important thing."

"Sure." Ryan's tone was as brutal as a slap across the mouth. "Do you want her to help me get him out?"

Ross's face drained white, and that was a hating in his eyes. He jumped down into the hole beside Ryan, and his eyes flicked about at the crumbled walls. The nervousness left him as he saw that what Ryan had said was true. The walls had fallen all they were going to.

They had to dig Oakes out to the knees before they could drag him free. He was amazed at his weakness. It took effort to stand and more effort to walk. His grin had a shamefaced tinge. "I guess I'd like to sit down for a little bit."

They led him to the shade of a tree, and Josie was twisting at her hands. "Oakes, what can I do?"

He looked at her in surprise. "Why, nothing, Josie." It was over with, and there was no need for anybody to do anything. But he saw how hard reaction was hitting her. The sheen of tears was in her eyes, and in a moment she was going to burst out crying.

"Josie, you can do something for me. Get me a drink. I didn't realize I was so dry."

She turned and flew toward the tent. If she fell at that pace, she would break her neck.

Ryan shifted his weight from one foot to the other. He was well aware of Oakes's displeasure with him.

Sitting here glaring at him was fine repayment for what Ryan had just done for him, and a grin warmed Oakes's face.

"Ryan, words can't say thanks."

"Then don't try it."

Oakes blew out a relieved breath. "All right. I won't." He was never a clever man with words. "How come you were here at the exact time I needed you?"

Ryan also showed relief that they were through the sticky moment. "I was on my way over to ask if you wanted to go to the meeting tonight. You've got big lungs. I heard you quite a way off."

"And you've got good legs." Those legs had carried Ryan here fast enough to turn that desperately needed split second in Oakes's favor. "What's the meeting about?" It made no difference. If Ryan wanted him to go, he was going.

That was the dark, smoky color of passion in Ryan's eyes. "The valley. It's time we decide where we're going. Fessler brought me word that the court's decided in the railroad's favor. We want as many people there tonight as we can get."

This took it out of the realm of doing a favor for Ryan. It was Oakes's business, too; his and Ross's. He turned his head toward his brother. "You're coming with us?"

Ryan's eyes flickered at the question, but he didn't comment.

Ross scraped at the ground with the side of his boot. "I'd better stay with Josie?"

Oakes had to choke off his words. They could take Josie with them. She had interest in this land; she would want to know what was going on. But he couldn't say it—not in front of Ryan. Ryan had seen enough disagreement in the Paulson family already.

Ryan looked relieved that Oakes wasn't going to argue. "I'll pick you up about six. That all right?"

Oakes nodded. He wanted Ryan to leave; he had some questions he had to ask Ross.

He waited until Ryan was out of hearing. "Why aren't you coming tonight? Damn it, Ross. Look at me."

That was a trace of wildness in Ross's face. "Because he doesn't want me along. And I'm trying to keep from quarreling with him. Didn't you see the way he looked at me?"

Oakes snorted. "He's got no disagreement with you."

Ross started to deny that, and his face crumbled. "I ran out on you, Oakes. He knows it. It's hard for him to be around me."

Something had broken through Ross's shell, for this was the first honest admission Oakes had heard him make in a long time. He climbed to his feet and put his arm about Ross's shoulders.

"You're letting it eat on you. Every man's got his weak spot. I've got a lot of fault in this. If I had remembered about the old cave-in, I wouldn't have asked you to help on the well."

Ross shook his head. "It happened a long time ago, Oakes. I should be over it by now."

"Forget it. When some mention of it comes up again with Ryan, I'll explain it to him."

Ross's eyes were cloudy. "I'm not sure I want that."

Oakes whacked him on the shoulder. "It'll work out. You'll see. Here comes Josie. There's no use troubling her." It had been a rare, good moment between them. He felt closer to Ross than he had in years, and the honesty had done that.

"Ross, are you sure you don't want to go to that meeting? It concerns you."

"I better hadn't, Oakes."

Oakes didn't push at his decision.

The meeting was held in the Grangeville schoolhouse, and about sixty settlers attended. John Morton was elected temporary chairman, and

Oakes saw his fumbling discomfort in the position. Neither Morton nor any of the others had a clear-cut idea of where he was going or how to set about it. Everybody tried to talk at once, and the words grew louder and angrier. The court's unfavorable decision was a tremendous setback to the settlers, and the disappointment and uncertainty were visible under the anger.

A man jumped to his feet in the rear of the room. "I say we make the railroad turn over our land to us right now. That land should have reverted back to the government." He was a big red-faced man, and his passion made his face a deeper hue. "The court has given the railroad permanent title to it, and they'll do anything they want with it. Including raising the price. I say we fight them."

"How do we go about that, Halderman?" another man asked.

"We march on that railroad office and show them we mean business. A show of force will change their minds in a hurry. All we've got to do is to stick together."

Oakes heaved himself to his feet. He had attended meetings before that had gone like this. It always happened when men had no clear purpose. They wrangled among themselves and wound up by screaming fight at everything and everybody. He almost grinned at himself. Galen Mundro should see him now. Hadn't Mundro picked him as a man of violence, violence which would attract other men? But violence because men could see no other course was always senseless to Oakes.

He held up a big hand. "Hold it. Hold it."

His size commanded attention, and rebellious voices muttered and died when that hard eye fixed them.

"Who are you going to fight?" he demanded. "One of the engines? Or its engineer?" He smiled frostily at the halfhearted chuckle that ran around the room. "The railroad is a big, impersonal thing. Who are you going to fight?"

"Are you saying let them do as they damn please?" Halderman yelled.

Morton pounded his palm for order. "The chair recognizes Dewey Halderman."

Halderman didn't care whether or not the chair recognized him. He had a mouthful of hot words, and he had to get them out. He stabbed a blunt finger at Oakes. "Do you know how much our irrigation ditches alone have added to the value of this land? Maybe half a million dollars. Do you think the railroad won't try to grab that value? They'll charge us for it, all right. My God! Haven't you seen enough of their lies and broken promises to know that? The court gives them land they're not entitled to, and you say don't fight them."

"I never said anything of the kind," Oakes

thundered. "I'm trying to tell you to pick a target and quit this blind shooting. The railroad has the court behind it, and the court is the law. That means the sheriffs, the marshals, the militia, and even the Army. Fight them, and you can be accused of starting a rebellion."

A subdued murmur ran through the room. Even Halderman's face was quieter. "Are you saying just give up?"

"Hell, no, I'm not giving up. I say organize. Organize into something so big the law has to listen to our voice, too. But do it all legal. Don't give the railroad a club to use against you."

He got a couple of grunts of approval, but more important, everybody was listening to him.

Halderman made an impatient gesture. "Go on."

"Appoint some of us to contact every settler in the valley. Make it plain we intend to make a legal fight for our land."

More approval sounded for him. "You'll need money. Every settler who joins should be assessed ten cents an acre. It'll amount to important money. And we'll need men with legal training to tell us how to go."

Several names were thrown at him, and he smiled. "We haven't even got a name for our organization yet."

"The Settlers' Land League," Halderman yelled, and a rising chorus of agreement filled the room. Faces turned toward Oakes, and he nodded. The name sounded all right to him.

Halderman flung up his hand for quiet. "Every man who joins must take a solemn oath to obey league officials without question, and above all other authority."

They liked that. Their shouts said so. Oakes roared against them until they were still. "No! That would set you up above anything else. Even the United States. Don't even talk about something like that, or the railroad could use it against you. You obey all the laws first. You need to draw up a constitution and elect your officials. And then talk over everything you plan to do before you take a step. You can't leave yourselves open. The railroad can take fifty punches from you without it hurting it. But one punch from them can floor you. You've got to always keep that in mind."

A heavy silence fell on the room, and Oakes thought he hadn't made himself heard. Then men began to nod thoughtfully.

Morton stood and cried, "I nominate—" He stared helplessly at Oakes; he didn't even know his name.

"Oakes Paulson," Ryan shouted.

Morton's voice picked up its volume. "Oakes Paulson for president of the league."

Oakes didn't hear a dissenting voice in the massed yelling. He tried to refuse by saying that none of them knew him, that he was a newcomer here, and he was beaten down. He looked around in bewilderment and sighed. "All right. Pick your other officers. We'll meet here a week from tonight." He turned and strode out of the building.

When Ryan joined him, Oakes was muttering to himself. "By God, I didn't want that. I had to say something. They were getting farther and farther off of the track."

Ryan grinned at him. "They picked the right man."

"We'll see. That Halderman wasn't the right one. He's a hothead, and he could be dangerous."

They climbed up into the wagon, and Ryan picked up the reins. "You've got him under control now."

Oakes wondered if a man ever controlled a Halderman. Damn, but he hadn't wanted this at all, but he had it now, and he would have to make the best of it.

Ryan snapped the reins for a little more speed. "You starting that well again tomorrow?"

"Thinking about it."

"You hold off until I get there."

"You've done enough. It's about time I start taking care of myself."

Ryan laughed. "You hold off until I get there. You hear me?"

Oakes stared straight ahead. If he had had a choice, he couldn't have picked a better neighbor.

He had been sitting here regretting being drawn into this new organization, bemoaning the time it would take and hating the responsibilities it could entail. Maybe he should stop his complaining. Maybe it was time to start earning neighbors like Ryan.

Dackett moistened, then lit, the end of his cigar. He cocked his feet upon the edge of the desk and blew a smoke ring toward the ceiling. He watched its white plumpness. Only good Havana cigars made a ring like that.

"How many were at the meeting?"

Tom Greason stirred eagerly in his chair. He was disappointed Dackett hadn't offered him a cigar, but that was the way Dackett was. Sometimes he appeared not to notice a man was near him.

"Sixty, Quincy. I knew you'd want to know. I counted them for you."

Dackett nodded absent approval.

Greason waited. He had learned long ago that Dackett didn't want a man's opinion; he just wanted information; and then it was best to wait until he asked for it. And the information had better be accurate.

He looked at the cracked toes of his shoes and bewailed their condition. It wasn't eight months ago that he had purchased a new pair. He didn't know where the money went. Those few acres he had simply wouldn't support his wife and daughter. Females were always a luxury unless a man had a lot of money—like Dackett, for instance. He could support a high-flying woman like his wife. Greason resented her. She looked at a man like he was dirt. He would like to have her for one night. He would put some respect in her. That thought always put a tingle in him.

"Greason! Are you listening to me?"

That put fright in Greason's face. He couldn't make it if it wasn't for the occasional handout Dackett gave him. He certainly didn't want to offend the man.

His face begged Dackett's pardon. "I missed that question, Quincy."

"Did Paulson work for that job?"

Greason frowned in appraisal. "I think they just up and elected him. He looked kinda surprised."

"Why did they elect him? He's not that well known yet."

"Some of them were talking fight, about marching on the railroad, and he calmed them down."

Dackett drew on his cigar. "I wonder if I've made a mistake with him?" He mused on it for a moment longer. "Well, I've undone mistakes before." So this Paulson had an appeal to men. They had listened to him tonight. It might be smart to start whittling on him now, before he grew any bigger.

His tone crispened. "Greason, I think you'd better keep your ears open for every lawless act that's committed around here. Any burnings, robberies, beatings, anything of that nature that's done by this new lawless organization. I'll keep Henshaw busy investigating them, and it'll put strain on Paulson." The decent people in the valley wouldn't like all that lawlessness, and wouldn't they blame the head of the organization that was doing it? He had another club to use against Paulson. He smiled as the gears began to mesh. He would discredit the Settlers' Land League with the decent people, and he would discredit Paulson with the league itself. That would be kicking all of the support out from under it, and nothing could stand that way.

Greason watched the smile grow on his face. Dackett was pleased with him. He could probably get a small loan from him tonight. He cleared his throat, made a false start, and cleared it again.

Chapter Ten

The flowing water in the irrigation ditch fascinated Oakes. It had been turned on three days ago, and he had been out here every minute he could afford, and a good many he couldn't. It touched the corner of his land, and he would have to dig the laterals himself, but that wouldn't be too great a job. He loved the color of the water, a pale green with perhaps a tinge of blue in it, and he loved the song it sang. It murmured sweetly as it moved between its sandy banks, promising the riches it would bring to this land.

He had a million things to be doing, and still he lingered. Actually he could afford this time, for he was ahead in work. The well was dug and producing. Ryan had brought a half-dozen men when he came the morning after the night of the meeting. And despite Oakes's protests, they had pitched in on the well. No, he couldn't blame his membership in the league for costing him ill-afforded time. He was way ahead of the game, for Ryan had brought more men the following week, and after two weeks of labor the house was framed in and the roof on. It needed a tremendous amount of work to finish it, but Josie was happy with it the way it was. Every time she looked at it, the radiance in her eyes was a marvelous thing.

Ryan had overriden Oakes's objections about the work these men were doing. "Don't you think they want to do it? Maybe they feel as though they're repaying something, too. You've given them a sense of direction and purpose, and a hope of winning. You go on and tend the league's business. We're tickled to catch up your work for you."

But even accepting that everything Ryan said was true, Oakes couldn't go on accepting their work. Not until in his own mind he was in a better position to pay them back. He was overpoweringly grateful to them for what they had done. They had lifted crushing pressure from him and let him see daylight ahead. It was a fortunate thing he had accepted Ryan's invitation to go to that first meeting.

The day was hot, and the more he looked at and listened to the water, the more beguiling it became. The chances of anybody coming along were almost nonexistent. He undressed, draped his clothes over a scrubby bush, then waded into the water. The surface was warm, heated by the sun, but just an inch or two below, the water carried the coldness of the mountain crest. Oakes sucked in his breath, then let out a ringing, "Woooo." The ditch was only chest deep, and as he waded into it his flesh became more numbed. It took action to offset it, and he rolled and swam, dived and came up to roll again. He blew out a stream of water. A man couldn't ask for better living than this.

Reta Dackett followed the irrigation ditch until she heard the splashing ahead of her. Every few seconds a joyous yell rang out, and she smiled at the sound of them. The woman back there at the unfinished house had said she might find Oakes at the irrigation ditch. That woman hadn't liked her; it had been in the flash in her eyes, and it had amused Reta. She knew that the woman was Oakes's sister-in-law, and that her status shackled her. She might not know it, but she was jealous of Oakes. It took another woman to see it. That was the basis of her dislike of Reta Dackett. She could be a pretty thing, if her clothes didn't make her look so drab. Reta had a small curiosity as to how Oakes felt about her. It didn't matter. He was shackled, too.

The ditch curved up ahead, and when she came around it she saw the man playing in the water like a happy puppy. She stopped her horse and watched him, and her eyes glistened. He was completely oblivious to her presence, and she watched him unashamedly. She gasped at the span of his shoulders and the size of his arm muscles. He was built on a massive scale, and his chest and stomach were larded with muscle. She felt suddenly breathless, as though a long run were behind her.

Some instinct must have touched him, for he turned his head and saw her.

She smiled with delight as she saw the blood pour up from his neck and color his face. He ducked until only his head was above water.

"Why, Oakes," she mocked. "I do believe you're embarrassed."

"Get out of here," he roared.

"Why, no, Oakes. I'm enjoying myself."

His eyes burned as he understood she had tossed him a dare. "Suit yourself, but I'm coming out."

He had tossed the dare back to her, and her eyes sparkled. "I can't stop you." He was bluffing, and calling it would give her a small mastery. She laughed as she saw the indecisiveness loosen his face.

The indecisiveness fled. He moved slowly toward the bank, and his shoulders emerged from the water, followed by his torso. She watched intently as the water ran in little rivulets from him, then broke up into drops.

He was out of the water to his waist, and still he came. He wasn't bluffing; he meant what he said.

"Wait!" The word came out as a faint squeak, and she hated that. "I'll leave. But I'm not going far. I want to talk to you. Will you call me when you're dressed?"

His eyes had never left her face, and she felt

the blood heat it. Damn him, she raged. She had lost in this exchange, and both of them knew it.

He grinned at her. "I'll call you."

She came back to the ditch at his hail. His hair was plastered to his skull, and his shirt stuck to his back. Apparently he had no way of drying himself.

He had a disconcerting way of staring at her. An odd little thought crossed her mind; could any woman break him to her will? Instantly, she answered it. Bend him perhaps, but break him never. But it would be an interesting war to try, though, for war it would be.

"What did you want to talk to me about, Mrs. Dackett?"

"My friends call me Reta."

"Do you always make friends this fast?"

Her breathing quickened. He was going to be a most irritating man. He intended giving her no help at all.

"Sometimes I do. Oakes, why can't we be friends?"

She had the impression he blinked, but it was a fleeting thing.

"You're a remarkably beautiful woman, Mrs. Dackett."

"I didn't think you'd noticed." That sounded too archly said, and she wished it hadn't slipped out.

"But friendship usually has some kind of a basis, doesn't it?"

She couldn't keep her face from flaming. The stubborn, infuriating fool. "I came out here to offer you some well-meant advice."

He allowed himself a sardonic grin. "Most advice falls in that classification."

She rushed her words out. She had to, or she would tear into him. "Oakes, don't fight the railroad. It isn't smart."

What a maddening way he had of weighing her words.

"Why isn't it smart?"

"Because you can't win. Can't you see that? A wise man picks the winning side."

"A lot of people have joined the league, Mrs. Dackett. Maybe enough to change things."

She shook her head in a pitying gesture. "They won't. The railroad is beginning to grade the land. They'll price it soon. Oakes, do you realize you might be able to price your own land?"

"Did Dackett send you?"

"No." That was true to a degree. He hadn't picked out today. "Why would he send me?"

"To offer me the bribe you just did. You've answered your question about why we can't be friends. We're on opposite sides."

She wanted to use her riding crop on him. "You are a fool."

A grin spread over his face. "You can't claim credit for discovering it."

His face sobered as she wheeled her horse and slashed it into a dead run. The league must be worrying Dackett, to send his wife out here like this. He stared after her. She was a remarkably pretty woman. The loneliness stirred and came to life again.

Josie settled herself on the wagon seat beside Oakes. "You've been sour ever since you returned from the irrigation ditch. Did something happen between you and your woman?"

He gave her a raking glance. "You know better than that. She's Dackett's wife. I'm sour because Ross promised to take you shopping. Where is he?"

She laid an apologetic hand on his arm. "I'm sorry, Oakes. I'm angry at him and taking it out on you. I don't know where he is."

It's starting again, he thought bleakly. Ross simply couldn't stay hitched for too long a time. Damn him. They had a good start here; they had promise and hope. If Ross messed this up, Oakes would break his neck. Ross hadn't told either of them where he was going, and that put a suspicious air to it.

Josie listened to the noise of the wagon. "It sounds solid, Oakes."

"It is. It was a good buy." It was second-hand,

but Oakes had checked it over, and was satisfied with it.

"What did your lady want?" A woman never forgot about an unanswered question.

"Dackett sent her with a bribe to get me to switch to the railroad. But it doesn't make sense—" He stopped and shook his head.

"What doesn't make sense?"

"That a man would send his wife on an errand like that. And why?"

"Maybe he didn't send her."

He gave her an astonished glance. "What are you talking about?"

Her face was angry. "Nothing, Oakes. Nothing at all. And I don't want to talk about it anymore."

He had a responsive anger that leaped to meet hers. That suited him just fine. He put his attention on his driving.

He drove into Hanford without further talk. He jerked the team to a sudden stop that snapped Josie's head forward and back. She glared at him. But he had noticed Galen Mundro across the street. Mundro had said he would be down in this country, but when he hadn't come, Oakes had pushed him to the back of his mind.

He stood and yelled, "Mundro."

Mundro looked toward him, and a delighted grin spread over his face. He bounded out into the street and reached up to take Oakes's hand. "Oakes, it's good to see you."

Oakes returned the handshake and pleasure with equal fervor. "And it's good to see you, Galen. When did you get in?"

"Yesterday afternoon. From what I hear things may be ready to heat up."

Oakes's face was grave. "They could be, Galen. My God, I've needed somebody like you to talk to."

Josie made an impatient stir at his side, and Oakes remembered his manners. "This is Josie Paulson, my sister-in-law. Josie, Galen Mundro. He's a newspaper man. Don't tell him anything you want kept secret. He's completely unreliable."

Mundro bowed low over her hand. "When I heard him say Josie Paulson, I thought you might be his wife. I should have known a woman as pretty as you could never listen to a man as ugly as he."

"Do you see what I mean?" Oakes demanded.

Her face held a rosy touch. "So far, I find him entirely reliable. Are you going to stay long, Mr. Mundro?"

"As long as it takes to do a job."

"Have you got time to talk to me now?" Oakes asked.

Mundro nodded.

"Good. Take Josie over to Kimberly's." He pointed at the restaurant across the street. "I'll be there as soon as I find a place for the team and wagon."

He watched them cross the street and noticed that several other people were observing it too. The town was filling up with doubts. People's nerves must be honed pretty fine if a body couldn't be seen with a newcomer without being suspect.

He joined Josie and Mundro, and said again, "I am glad to see you."

Mundro smiled at Josie. "In Sacramento he wasn't. I had a feeling about him the first time I saw him. I tried to enlist him in a cause, and he wouldn't even listen."

Josie's bad temper seemed to be gone, and her manner said she liked this man. She smiled back at him. "Causes have a way of enlisting him. One has here."

Mundro bobbed his head. "I've heard a little about it." He grinned at Oakes. "I never figured you for a peacemaker."

Oakes ordered lemonade for them, and Mundro changed his order to coffee. "A lot of them were ready to march, Galen. I just couldn't see where we could gain by it."

"I preached violence to you, Oakes, but you handled it right. The first overt move toward the railroad, and it would call in state militia. The governor might even have an excuse to yell for federal troops. He's a strong railroad man. Then you'd be stopped before you got started. The way I see it is a slow step at a time and build up public opinion until it favors us."

Oakes nodded gloomily. "But some of the settlers don't see it that way. I've got a few who are fighting me to turn the league loose against the railroad." Briefly, he talked about Halderman. "He drilled a mounted squadron of troops in Lemoore last night. I got one report of thirty men, another of forty. He insists he's not going to stand still and be taken by surprise."

Mundro squinted at him. "I'd say your Halderman was a Southern officer." He laughed as Oakes nodded. "It's typical. Too much fire and too little brains. If he led your league, all the railroad would have to do is sit back and let him make the mistakes."

Kimberly brought the order, and Oakes paid for it. He waited until Kimberly was out of earshot and sighed. "A man doesn't know who to trust anymore. Every lawless act is being blamed on the league. The local paper hammers on the theme that this is a lawless organization, and that its leaders are ordering these crimes. It's got the people who haven't joined us wondering about us."

Mundro nodded. "Good propaganda. I gather the local paper's taking railroad money?"

"Everything they print is favorable."

"Proof enough." Mundro stirred his coffee absently. "Oakes, you can't just go on letting them accuse you without doing something about it."

Oakes spread his hands helplessly. "Halderman's been after me to let him turn his squadron loose on the paper. He wants to wreck it. He claims masks will disguise them."

Mundro slapped the table with his palm. "He is a fool. Give the railroad violence they can react against, and they'll tear the lid off of hell."

"He's building up favor. Some of the members are beginning to say I just sit around and do nothing."

"Have you tried to run down one of those crimes and find out who actually committed it?"

Oakes shook his head, and excitement shone in Mundro's eyes. "Then that's our first step." He smiled at Oakes's expression. "You can't see what good it will do? You have a local printer besides the paper? Fine, fine. We'll get our story printed on handbills and distribute them. We won't make as big a yell as the paper, but we'll be heard." His enthusiasm lessened. "But that will take money. And I'm fresh out of that commodity."

The enthusiasm merely transferred from Mundro's face to Oakes's. "I can get you the money, Galen. We made an assessment and haven't spent any of it. You'll need help?"

"I'll call for it when I do." Mundro stood and finished the last of his coffee. He made a wry face. "I let it get cold. I'll let you know about the help later. Josie, it's been my pleasure." He bowed and wheeled toward the door. He moved like a man in a hurry.

"Josie. I'm glad he's here. I needed a smarter head than the one I've got. He doesn't look it, but he's tough. And he doesn't scare worth a damn."

"I like him." Her tone was decisive. "And if we don't get that shopping done, we won't get home 'fore dark."

Oakes agreed with her. He would like to get back and save the last hour of daylight.

He carried Josie's purchases out to the wagon, then looked back and frowned. He had thought she was right behind him, but she was talking to some woman just outside the store. The woman was shabbily dressed, and there was the shadow of privation in her plain face. She wore a beaten, hopeless air, and Oakes had the feeling she mentally wrung her hands every few minutes. He wondered if the girl beside her was her daughter. She looked to be thirteen or fourteen years old, big for her age and well developed, and his frown deepened. Her parents were going to have to start dressing her differently; she was no longer a kid. She was as shabbily dressed as the woman, and Oakes had the feeling there was something not quite right about her. Her eyes shifted too quickly, and when they did stop on something, they rested there too long and too vacantly.

He shifted impatiently while he waited for

Josie to finish her conversation. He was losing good daylight.

He saw Josie press the woman's hand, pat the girl on the shoulder, then move to him. He waited until he got the team started. "Who was that?"

"Abigail Greason. Tom Greason's wife."

Oakes knew him by sight. Abigail Greason didn't have much of a bargain. "That their daughter?"

"Yes. I feel so sorry for them. He drinks everything away. I don't see how they live. Letty is fourteen, and I don't believe she's had two years' schooling."

"She's not right, is she?" At Josie's indignant glance he defended himself. "Well, she doesn't look right."

"I don't think she is," Josie admitted. "But she's had no chance. Oakes, why do some men drag their families down with them?"

He shook up the team. Who could answer that? It was a sobering thought, but every action a man took, good or bad, had its reflecting reaction on somebody else.

Chapter Eleven

"Damn you," Oakes yelled, and heaved his driving stick at the darting hog. Off to his left he heard Ryan's impassioned cursing. Trying to drive hogs would put the devil in a saint. The goddamned perverse, stubborn creatures. They didn't have much endurance, but for several yards they moved like greased lightning. They could dart like rabbits, and reverse direction just as quickly. When a man finished moving hogs, his lungs were pumping and his legs trembling. And he had no good humor left in him.

Oakes made a quick dash to cut off a hog that had a break in its head, and sent it streaking back to the bunch. He wished he could get close enough to kick it.

The lead hog saw the hole in the fence and scampered through it. The rest followed it, and they had the damned things back inside the fence. Oakes wiped his face. He and Ryan had been the better part of two hours getting those hogs penned up again. And they couldn't stop now and rest no matter how much outraged leg muscles screamed for it. Four holes in the fence had to be repaired.

Ryan's face had a grim set as he worked at mending one of the holes. Oakes stood guard over the other three, making short dashes from one hole to the other, scaring the hogs from them. Once a hog got an idea in its head, it couldn't be knocked out with a club. They would keep trying to get out those holes until they were repaired.

Ryan finished and flung his hammer toward his tool shed. Oakes watched in surprise. He had never seen Ryan display this much temper.

He took hold of Ryan's arm. "We'd better get a drink of water and cool off."

Ryan glared at him. "Oakes, those holes were cut. It's happened before. I've lost hogs I couldn't get back in."

"You sure, Ryan?"

"I'm damned sure." Ryan stopped at the well and drew up a bucket of water. He filled a dipper and handed it to Oakes. He drank his fill, then poured part of the bucket over his head. Oakes did the same and felt cooler. Ryan didn't look any cooler.

He sat down beside Ryan in a live oak's shade. "Tell me about it."

"I made a bad mistake, Oakes. I borrowed money from Dackett because I could get it from him faster than anybody else. And hogs are a quick way to market. Six months, and I have my profit. But at the rate it's going, I'm not going to get them to market. Dackett wouldn't take the hogs as security. I put up my land."

A man was always crazy to put up his land

unless there was no other way out. Every farmer knew that. Evidently Ryan had had no other way out.

Ryan picked up a handful of sand and let it sift through his fingers. "I was hoping to have them ready in two or three weeks. Who else would be interested in seeing that I don't make it? I tell you the man's a hog himself. No matter how much he gobbles up he wants more."

"We'll see these hogs are sold whenever you want them to be."

Ryan gave Oakes a grateful glance. "I'm glad you happened by this morning. I'd have spent most of the day trying to round them up by myself."

"This has happened before?"

"Five or six times. I know Dackett hired somebody to cut my fences. I wish to God I could catch them at it."

"Where are you going to sell them?"

"San Francisco, if I can get them there. Dackett's turned the screw a little harder on me there. I stopped at the railroad office and asked for freight rates. You wouldn't believe the rate they quoted me. The clerk said hogs were something new for them to ship, and the rates had to be high to be sure they didn't lose money. Dackett set those rates, and he made damned sure he wouldn't leave me anything."

Oakes had heard complaints from other

shippers—the wheat growers, the fruit and vegetable raisers. When it looked as though a man was going to make a decent profit on his crop, the railroad stepped in and trimmed all the profit away.

"Why do you want to go to San Francisco with them?"

"They're in great demand by the Orientals. I can get almost double for them there."

Oakes nodded. That was good and sufficient reason. "Then we'll drive them there."

Ryan snorted. "Do you know how far it is to San Francisco? Have you forgotten the trouble we just had with them?"

"I wasn't intending just two of us doing it. We'll have to get more men."

"It'll take a lot. Since the no-fence law was passed a man is held responsible for the damage his stock does."

"You mean if his stock breaks into a field?"

"Even if it's an open fence. The law was passed to keep a landowner from having to fence. You keep your stock on the road, or you pay."

Oakes's face was thoughtful. That was going to take a lot of men, but Ryan gave readily of time and work, and he asked no repayment of anybody. He had a few requests of his own coming to him.

"Ryan, I'll announce at the meeting tonight that we need drovers for hogs." He chuckled with sudden mirth. "I'll bet it'll be the first such drive California's seen."

Ryan's face crinkled, and he stared off to one side for a long moment.

Oakes touched his knee. "I'll let Galen tell about it. He can stir up people pretty good."

Ryan could trust himself again. "He must be driving Dackett crazy."

"He sure stopped the league from being blamed for every crime that happened around here."

Ryan laughed in sudden delight. "And he put Henshaw to work."

They grinned at each other in mutual pleasure. It had taken Mundro a little over a week to find out who was behind those crimes. Perhaps not actually who was behind them, but who had committed them. The robberies in town had been committed by a couple of town loafers, and Mundro had enough proof on them in a few days so that Henshaw had to arrest them. Some of the stock disappearances and the barn burnings he had tracked to full or part-time railroad workers, and that pointed the finger at Dackett. Mundro distributed his handbills so that everybody in the valley got a chance to read them. The local paper could scream fraud until it was red in the face, but the proof was in Henshaw's jail. The local paper was a liar, plain and simple.

Oakes knew that Mundro's work had given the league new life. Membership was up over four hundred men, and even Halderman had toned down his belligerence. Mundro was spending most of his time with a lawyer now, and the settlers hoped not to be as defenseless in court as they had been.

Ryan shook his head in admiration. "He doesn't look that tough, does he?"

Oakes stood and dusted off his seat. "He doesn't. When do you think we ought to plan the drive? Three weeks?"

Before Ryan could answer, the pound of hooves jerked his head around. "It's Josie. And she seems to be in a hurry."

She was. She rode bareback on Oakes's heavy work horse, and she demanded all the speed it had. Oakes lunged to help her dismount, and he was too slow. She displayed a lot of calf as she jumped off.

Urgency was in the clutch of her fingers on his arm. "They've got Galen in jail."

He stared stupidly at her. "What for?"

She shook her head. "Mrs. Meadows didn't know. But she just came from town, and she says he's locked up."

Oakes and Ryan exchanged hard glances. Oakes blew a heavy breath. "I guess we'd better go in. We were congratulating ourselves too soon. Dackett wasn't going to take that pushing around from Mundro without hitting back."

"I'm going," Josie said firmly.

She bristled at the expression on his face. "He's my friend, too."

"Come on, then," Oakes said, and sighed. "Is Ross home?"

The familiar pinched look about her lips gave him his answer.

A milling crowd was before the jail when they arrived. At the moment it sounded more noisy than anything else, but Oakes knew how quickly that could turn. Whatever it was, was pulling a lot of people.

He handed the reins to Ryan. "You and Josie wait here. I'll see if I can find out what it's about."

He climbed down and shouldered his way through the crowd. Somebody called, "Wait until you hear what your big-city friend has done."

The condemnation in his voice was reflected in the faces about him. A few nights ago they had cheered Mundro. Whatever it was had to be pretty bad to swing them over this fast. He saw men on opposite sides of the land question now mingling, their animosity toward one another lost in some common indignation.

He kept his face and voice mild as he pushed his steady way toward the building. "Later, later," he kept repeating, as hands reached out to detain him. He could ask any of them what Mundro had done, but he wanted the official version; he wanted it from Henshaw.

Henshaw blocked him out of the building. "No one allowed inside." He cradled a shotgun, and two deputies backed him up. Oakes knew Bill Whelen; the other was a new man.

"Is Mundro in there?"

Henshaw's face looked swollen with malice. "He is. And I never saw a man who deserved it more."

"What's he done?"

"You'll find out when he's tried. Unless the crowd doesn't think he deserves a trial. I wouldn't blame them if they took justice in their own hands."

It was an ugly answer. It meant that Henshaw wouldn't make the slightest effort to protect Mundro. If this crowd turned into a mob and made a serious surge at the jail, Oakes had no doubt Henshaw and his deputies would flee out of the rear door.

He stared hard at the sheriff. "Henshaw, doesn't it gag you to see your face in a mirror?"

He turned his back on Henshaw's spluttering. He would have to get his information from someone in the crowd, and he tried to pick out somebody who seemed the least swept along by the event. He asked John Morton, and Morton shook his head.

"It's a bad thing, Oakes. He's been molesting children."

"Oh, my God," Oakes exploded, and Morton

took it as a mark of Oakes's shock and disgust. "It's true, all right, Oakes. Henshaw has full proof."

"Morton, you're a goddamned fool."

Morton's face reddened. "I don't have to have my nose rubbed in it to be able to identify it."

Anger lengthened Oakes's strides back to the wagon. He climbed into it so angry he couldn't speak.

Josie's face was anxious. "What is it, Oakes?"

Oakes shook his head at her. Clay Dunning was the lawyer Mundro had been working with, and Oakes couldn't trust himself to talk about it, not until after he had discussed it with Dunning. He drove a couple of blocks and stopped before Dunning's office.

Dunning was a short, fat man with shrewd eyes. He had a habit of running his palm over his bald head, then inspecting it for moisture. Oakes considered him an honest man.

"Clay, you know Josie?"

Dunning nodded to her and Ryan. "Sit down, sit down." Something shadowed his eyes.

"You've been to the jail, Oakes?" Dunning nodded at Oakes's reply. "Then you already know."

It looked as though Dunning thought there was something to it, and the thought drove Oakes frantic. "You don't believe it?"

Dunning exploded. "No, I don't believe it. I

got to know Mundro pretty well. But it doesn't make a damned bit of difference what you and I believe." He waved his arm. "They believe it."

"Believe what?" Josie cried.

Dunning didn't try to soften it. "Galen Mundro has been arrested for child molestation."

Her face went shocked. "No," she whispered. "Who?"

"Tom Greason's daughter. Henshaw stopped him from killing Mundro. Greason acted enough like it was true."

Oakes leaned toward him. "Have you talked to Galen?"

"Henshaw wouldn't let me get close. Oakes, I've been going crazy, watching that crowd build up. I was down there just a few minutes ago, and it's double the size it was an hour ago. I picked out a half-dozen men who are stirring it up with talk about little children and why wait for justice to drag its feet. They've picked the one thing that will drive a bunch of men crazy, crazy enough to take matters into their own hands."

"They? Who do you mean?"

"Who's the man who benefits most with Mundro off his back?"

"Dackett!"

Dunning nodded. "It's to his benefit to keep that crowd at a high pitch. I predict the very least they'll do to Galen is to tar and feather him and ride him out of town on a rail. Dackett would be happy enough to settle for that."

Oakes remembered his earlier estimation of the Greason girl. "I don't think that Greason girl is bright."

"Probably not. But that works against Mundro. People are saying it made it easier for him—" He broke off and colored. "Pardon me, Josie."

She stood, and Oakes thought, She's too shocked to take more of this. When she asked to take the wagon for a while, he was glad to let her have it. A woman had no part in a discussion like this.

He waited until the door closed behind her. "Clay, have you tried to talk to Greason?"

Dunning gave him a withering glance. "No, I've just sat here on my ass and done nothing."

"Ah, Clay, I put it badly."

Dunning was partially appeased. "I tried to find him when this thing broke. He isn't home, and his wife doesn't know where he is. I believe her. I've been back there twice. He isn't there. Greason is a hard drinker. Dackett's smart enough not to trust a drunk. He'll have him in a safe place."

Oakes looked at Ryan. He was getting scared. Ryan had that same uneasy look on his face. He looked back at the lawyer. "Clay, tell us what to do."

Dunning's face was heavy with hopelessness. "You tell me. Don't you think I've been racking my brains all day? There's not one damn thing we can do, Oakes. Our own people are in that crowd."

Oakes pounded the desk in his helplessness. "They're not going to take him."

Dunning sighed. "Just tell me how to stop them."

Oakes stood, and Ryan joined him. "We'll stop them some way." The look now on Ryan's face equaled the determination in Oakes's voice.

"You'll get yourself killed," Dunning cried. "Just give Henshaw the slightest excuse, and he'll blast you."

"We'll see." Oakes started for the door, Ryan on his heels.

Dunning reached for his hat. "I'm going with you, though I don't know how a man keeps another from putting his neck in a noose when he's determined to do it."

The late afternoon hours were long and hot. Oakes saw the thing that Dunning had mentioned: men working the crowd to a higher pitch. The crowd was big enough to block off the street in front of the jail now. The setting sun scorched the scene, and tempers grew edgier under it. The crowd was working itself up at a faster pitch. Every now and then men broke into explosive yells, all directed at Mundro.

It'll happen about dark, or a little after, Oakes thought. He knew the kind of action it would be. He had tried a dozen times to talk sense into individual heads, and not a one had listened to him. He wished he and Ryan had guns; they would stop these fools. Dunning had been horrified when Oakes suggested they buy them.

"The worst thing you could do, Oakes. Showing a gun would be suicide. If Henshaw didn't drop you, the crowd would roll over you. Do you want to be the one who sets it off?"

No, Oakes didn't want that. But he knew one thing. If the crowd started toward the jail, he was going to be between it and the building.

Abigail Greason had been so pleased to see Josie. She bustled about, clearing the clutter from the chairs in the parlor so that Josie could sit down. She wasn't very efficient, for she did several things over.

Josie watched her futility. She thought that Abigail Greason fought life with the same aimlessness.

Abigail apologized profusely for being able to offer only water, and Josie said that water would be fine. She listened to Abigail's runaway chatter and thought, Poor thing. She has so few visitors. It showed in Abigail's craving for talk.

She heard Letty singing out in back; it was a happy, empty sound.

"Letty," Abigail called. "Mrs. Paulson's here."

Josie had an ugly subject, and she didn't know

how to approach it. She took a deep breath and plunged in. "What a horrible thing to have happen to Letty. She wasn't harmed?"

"She was lucky. She was able to break away from him and run. I thought my heart would stop when I heard about it. And I was sure Tom was going to shoot the monster."

"Terrible, terrible," Josie murmured.

Letty came into the room and walked over to Josie, holding out her hand. "What did you bring me today?"

"Letty!" Abigail's face was shocked.

"She always brings me something, doesn't she?"

Josie laughed at her directness. In the past, she had brought trinkets for Letty. "Nothing today, Letty. But I'll make up for it next time."

She expected the child's face to fall, and was relieved when it didn't.

Letty shrugged. "I don't care. I've got a new dress and shoes. Do you want to see them?"

"Yes, I do, Letty."

Josie properly admired the new clothing. "Why did you get them, Letty? It isn't a holiday."

"Tom bought them for her. Because of the scare she went through." Abigail's face turned resentful. "Though we could have used the money for something else." She unconsciously raised her hand almost to her cheek.

Josie wondered if she had said the same thing

to her husband and had taken a blow for it.

This could be a cruel thing to do, but it had to be done. "Letty, tell me about your scare."

Abigail looked indignant, then it faded. Mrs. Paulson was about the only friend they had.

Letty's eyes looked dreamy and far away. "The bad man promised me candy if I would come with him to Mr. Creighton's shed in back of his store. The shed was empty and dark. The man put his hand under my dress, then tried to make me take it off. He scared me. I broke away from him and ran."

"How awful, Letty. Would you tell me again?"

Abigail seemed startled, and opened her mouth to protest. But Letty was already talking. She was happy to be the center of attention.

She told it exactly the same way she had told it the first time. Josie hadn't written it down, but she was sure not a word had been changed.

Josie sent the girl out to play, then faced Abigail. "She's lying, Abigail. She told that story exactly the same way both times. No child will do that."

Abigail's face was furious. "Well," she snapped. "I never heard of such a thing. If that's the way you feel, you can leave."

"Abigail, listen to me. A man can be hanged because of Letty's story. Do you want that? If it's a false story, the hanging will be on your shoulders. You're a Christian woman. If you can prevent this hanging and you don't—" Josie broke off, watching Abigail's face intently. She was convinced that Letty was lying, and its origin came from her father. If Abigail was also a part of the plot, then Josie was lost. But she had to gamble that Abigail knew nothing of it.

"Your responsibility will last the rest of your life, Abigail. If the truth comes out, it won't lessen your guilt because you didn't know then. You can prove or disprove it now. Call Letty back and ask her to repeat the story. Give me a pencil and paper. This time I'll write it down so you can check it."

She thought the woman was going to refuse, and she watched her tear herself apart with indecision. "Abigail, don't you want to free your mind and soul?"

Abigail drew a deep breath and raised her voice. "Letty."

Letty didn't mind telling her story again. She considered it part of a game and enjoyed it. Josie scribbled furiously, then handed the paper to Abigail.

She reached out and took hold of Letty's hand. "Letty, I'll bet you can't tell your story again."

"I can too."

Letty plunged into her mechanical recitation, and Abigail's eyes followed the words on the paper. When Letty finished, Abigail's face was white.

"Was it the same?" Josie already knew; the answer was in Abigail's face.

"She did memorize it."

Josie bobbed her head. "Yes, Abigail. I don't know why. Maybe she was promised the dress and shoes if she did."

Abigail sank to her knees and held Letty tightly to her. "Honey, Mama isn't going to be mad at you, if you tell me the truth. But that man never touched you, did he?"

"Yes, he did." Letty started to go into her recital again, and Abigail shook her. "I want you to tell me the truth."

"You'll take my dress and shoes away."

Josie leaned over and stroked her hair. "No, she won't. And I'll add a gift to it, if you tell us the truth. What did your papa give you the dress and shoes for?"

Letty's eyes bored into her face. "You'll let me pick out the gift?"

"I promise."

"Paw gave the dress and shoes to me for telling that story about that man. It was hard. I had to say it over and over until he thought I knew it. And he made me look at that man a dozen times until I was sure I had the right one." She giggled in sudden delight. "He was easy to remember. He wears funnier clothes than other men."

Josie hugged her in thankfulness. "Yes, Letty. He wears big-city clothes."

She straightened. It was getting dark outside, and she didn't know how much time she had left. It had taken time to drive out here, and much more time had been spent in getting the truth out of Letty. "Abigail, you know what we have to do?"

Abigail's face was pale, but she nodded. "Oh, yes. I'm ready whenever you are." Her hand closed convulsively on Letty's arm. "Poor thing, poor thing," she whispered.

"Yes," Josie said simply.

Oakes cursed the torches men lit and brought to the scene. Somehow, they made it worse. The flames flickered and danced in the breeze. They put an evil, inflamed shine on faces, turning them from known ones into those of complete strangers. There was much more shifting and stamping of feet and a steady yelling at Henshaw to turn him over.

Oakes looked at Ryan. "They won't hold much longer."

"Nope." Ryan looked calm enough, but there was a tightness about his eyes.

Dunning caught hold of Oakes's sleeve. "What are you thinking of?"

"I'm not rightly sure, Clay. Don't try to come with us. You'd only be in the way."

Dunning looked at him helplessly, then stepped back.

Oakes pushed through the crowd, and he wasn't gentle. Ryan followed right behind him, blocking anybody who showed too much resentment of Oakes's hands.

Oakes climbed the three steps, then faced the crowd. Ryan stood spraddle-legged beside him, a bright, dangerous-looking smile on his lips.

Oakes held up both hands until he got silence. "Listen to me. You can't judge the evidence. You're not trained for it. Taking the law into your own hands will only hurt you."

"Are you still trying to save your friend?" someone yelled.

Oakes threw a pugnacious look about him. "Who said that? If he's guilty, I'm as ready as anybody here to see him punished. But by a court. Not by any mob."

Halderman pushed out of the crowd and advanced to the bottom of the steps. "You might as well quit. You're not talking us out of anything."

"Just until morning," Oakes pleaded. "Give us a chance to cool our heads and look at the evidence again. Is that asking too much?"

Henshaw stepped out of the doorway. "It is. When a little girl tells you what this one told me, anything that favors the man who tried to assault her is asking too much."

Halderman's face twisted. "Get out of our way, Paulson." He bounded up the steps and seized

Oakes's arm, tugging on it. Oakes freed his arm and dragged Halderman to him. His other hand closed on the man, and he lifted him high. Halderman kicked and struggled, but Oakes held him aloft a moment.

"Goddamn it!" Oakes roared. "All I'm asking for is a little time."

He pitched Halderman from him, and a frightened squawk burst from the man's lips. He got good distance, and a half-dozen men went down under Halderman. A tangle of arms and legs threshed about on the ground, and the swearing was hot enough to scorch ears.

Awe held men motionless a moment. Then the rumbling started, rumbling that grew steadily into furious roaring. The roaring would be like a whip, slashing them forward, and the two men on the steps wouldn't be enough to make the wave falter.

"Oakes!" A clear voice rang out above the crowd noise. "Oakes." Josie stood in the wagon box. "I've got Mrs. Greason and Letty here. They want to say something. Will you clear a path for them?"

Oakes and Ryan plunged from the stoop, and again they knocked men out of the way. Josie just smiled at all of Oakes's questions.

The presence of the women created enough curiosity in the mob to hold it back for a moment. Oakes and Ryan cleared a narrow lane back to the stoop. Oakes handed up Josie and Mrs. Greason, and Letty bounded up beside her mother.

Josie looked over the crowd, and scorn showed on her face. "You were so ready to believe the flimsiest proof. You wouldn't give a man who was helping you a chance. Tell them, Letty."

Mrs. Greason placed her arm around Letty's shoulders and said something to her. Letty was very close to tears.

"I didn't tell the truth," Letty whimpered.

"Why didn't you tell the truth?" Josie prompted.

"Because Paw promised me a new dress and shoes."

"And why did he promise them?"

"If I'd tell a lie about the man who wears the funny looking clothes."

"He didn't touch you, Letty?"

Letty shook her head and burst into tears.

Josie said something to her mother, and Mrs. Greason put both arms about her daughter and started walking her back to the wagon. The crowd swayed back, giving her room, and not a man made a sound.

Josie's eyes flayed them. "You make me sick to look at you."

Halderman's face was upturned to her. "What were we to believe? We acted the best we thought—"

"Thought!" she cried. "There wasn't a thought among you. You were sheep, letting them push and shove you the way they wanted you to go. And you." She whirled on Henshaw. "You're supposed to be a sheriff. If those were men out there, they'd run you out of town."

"How else could I act?" Henshaw bleated. "The girl told me what sounded like a straight story. What else could I do?"

Oakes smiled fondly at her. Wasn't she something? He had always known there was fire in her, but not in this quantity. He had to get Mundro turned loose as quickly as possible. He wanted to find Greason and ask him some questions, and he wouldn't be gentle or patient in his questioning.

Dackett backed hastily into deeper shadow, and his eyes were bitter. One moment, everything had been going just as he wanted; the next, everything had crumbled. If he had only stopped that damned Paulson woman, but how could he have known why she was here? He hadn't seen the Greason woman and the girl until it was too late to stop them. Frustration was as keen as an actual knife slashing at his chest. That mob would have surged forward in another few seconds, and nothing could have stopped it. Mundro, Oakes, and Ryan. He had been so damned close to eliminating all three of them right here.

He could actually taste the sour burning in his throat. This night wasn't over yet, and it wouldn't be until he reached Greason. Oakes would be after Greason with questions as to why he had wanted his daughter to lie about Mundro. Dackett shivered as he thought of how long Greason could stand up against Oakes Paulson.

He had to walk three blocks before he reached his horse. He looked furtively around, and nobody was in sight. He mounted, and moved out of town at a slow walk. Only after he was a good distance away did he dare set the horse into a gallop. What was ahead had to be done fast and ruthlessly. The prospect didn't disturb him.

He rode some twenty minutes and stopped before a tumbledown shack. Lamplight shone faintly through a grimy window. He stepped quickly inside and shut the door behind him. Greason sat at a table, his head lolling from side to side. A half-filled bottle was before him, an empty one on the floor.

He was almost into oblivion, and he had to focus hard to recognize Dackett. "Quincy." His voice was slurred and almost inaudible. "Haven't left here. Did just like you told me. Have they hanged him yet?"

The question amused him, and he laughed. "Guess you showed him who's the smartest. He won't be bothering you anymore."

"Why, yes, he will, Tom." Dackett sounded easy and casual. "Probably even more than before. And you didn't do as I told you." Passion contorted his face. "You told your half-witted daughter why you gave her the dress and shoes, and you didn't tell your wife to keep her mouth shut."

Greason's mouth sagged open. "They wouldn't tell anybody, Quincy. I know they wouldn't."

Dackett fixed him with merciless eyes. "You know, do you, Tom? They already have. Henshaw has turned Mundro loose by now. And Paulson is looking for you to ask some questions. Wouldn't it be bad for me, Tom, if you told him I was behind all this?"

Greason made a frantic gesture. "You know I wouldn't do that, Quincy. Hell, he won't get a thing out of me." His eyes went wide with horror as Dackett tugged a gun from his pocket. "Don't, Quincy." His voice barely rose above a squeak. "I promise you—"

"Tom, you couldn't expect me to take a chance like that." Dackett pulled the trigger, and the bullet slammed Greason's head backward. For a moment he sat there, dazed surprise molding his face. As the blood started, he toppled sideways and fell to the floor.

Dackett moved to the door before he looked back. The bottle had fallen, too, and its contents were gurgling out onto the floor. He grinned bleakly. It seemed almost a shame that Greason hadn't had time to drink that.

Chapter Twelve

The court decision was a bomb, and its explosion left men dazed and reeling. The land in question belonged to the railroad; it could price it as it pleased. And if the railroad chose to take a man's improvements into consideration and increase the price of the land, that was within the railroad's province.

Oakes and Mundro were hard put to keep the league under control. Men wanted to march against the railroad office and tear it down; they wanted to run Dackett out of the country. Halderman yelled that his mounted squadron was ready, and he boasted how fast he could do the job.

Oakes called him on it in the street. "Are you insane, Halderman? Dackett's already got one United States marshal here. Don't you realize what that marshal has behind him?"

A sizable group of men were with Halderman, and their faces showed they thought as he did. "We're fighting for our homes now," Halderman bellowed. "We don't care what's against us."

"You use force on that marshal, and he can call in the Army and Navy. That's what's behind him."

Halderman made a savage slash of his hand.

"Let him call them in." He thrust his face close to Oakes's. "You're always counseling wait. And each day the railroad gets more powerful. Would you have a reason to be talking that way?"

Oakes eyed him steadily. "Say it plainer, Dewey."

"There's talk Mrs. Dackett is the reason you work against the league. She's caught your eye, and you can't see anything else."

Oakes would have hit him if Mundro hadn't grabbed his arm. The men with Halderman took Oakes's fury as proof that Halderman had uncovered his real purpose.

Mundro tugged him away, and Oakes yelled his protest at every step. "Hell, Galen, I haven't seen her in weeks." He had to think to recall the exact day. "Not since that day at the irrigation ditch."

Mundro's eyes were bright with speculation. "She rode quite a way to offer you something."

Oakes's face burned. "She advised me I was on the wrong side. Nothing more."

Mundro screwed up his face in thought. "But somebody's using her name to throw you in bad repute with the league. Tell a lie often enough, and it can be as effective as the truth. Halderman wants the league, Oakes. If he can discredit you, he can make his grab for power. A lot of them will listen to him. They can't see any progress we've given them."

"What can we do about it, Galen?"

"They won't listen to a denial, Oakes. You'll have to show them proof of it."

"Oh, my God. How can I do that?"

"I don't know." Mundro looked back. Halderman was haranguing the men. "But you'd better do it before you leave with Ryan on his drive. Or it could be completely out of control by the time you get back. Maybe it would be wiser not to go at all. Can't Ryan get somebody else?"

Oakes shook his head. Ryan would see the necessity of Mundro's proposal, and he would agree, but Oakes couldn't do it to Ryan; not after everything the man had done for him.

"All right, Oakes." A helpless note was in Mundro's voice. "I hope you can work it out, or somebody's going to get this valley bathed in blood."

Oakes thought about it on the way home. This thing was a snake, and it grew heads faster than a man could lop them off. He had no doubt Dackett was behind this new attack. He spat into the dust. But to use his wife's name—

A jolting, jarring bump shattered the rest of the thought. He felt its impact run through him, and the wagon canted at a crazy angle. For a moment he didn't realize what had happened; then he saw the wheel rolling down the road ahead of him. The wagon had been moving slowly, and the wheel didn't roll far before it wobbled and fell.

He didn't have to halt the team; the dragging

axle end was enough to do that. He swore as he climbed down to the road. He retrieved the wheel first, then came back and put a search on the road behind the wagon. He searched quite a while and finally found the wheel nut, and that relieved him. That nut could have rolled almost anyplace.

He leaned the wheel against the wagon near the down end of the axle. The wagon was heavy, but he could lift one corner of it. The trouble was that he couldn't hold it up while he maneuvered the wheel onto the axle. He tried several times before he was convinced he couldn't do it. He was going to have to walk home and get help, or wait until somebody came along.

This road wasn't traveled too often, and he didn't relish either a wait or a long walk. He heard the approach of a buggy while he was still deciding which course to take.

Reta pulled up alongside him. "Oakes! You're in trouble."

She regarded him with the same queer intensity that always made him uncomfortable.

"Can I help you, Oakes?"

He smiled at her. "Not unless you can put this wheel on the axle when I pick it up." It was heavy, and even if she considered touching it, he doubted she could manage it.

She climbed eagerly from the buggy. "I can try."

Now he wished he hadn't proposed it. He didn't

want to be under the slightest obligation to her.

"What do you want me to do?" She listened attentively as he gave his orders.

He placed the wheel as close to the axle's end as he could without it getting in his way. "Don't try to rush," he warned. "I can hold it." She could line up hub and axle. The difficult part would come when she had to lift the wheel a tiny fraction to slide it back as far as it would go on the axle. He doubted she had the strength for it.

He lifted the axle, and she rolled the wheel up until she had it lined up. She tried lifting the big wheel, and he could see its dirt staining her blouse and hands. The strain was beginning to hit them both. He could feel it stealing through his arms, and it showed up in the increased color in her face.

"It's too much," he panted. "Drop it."

Some stubborn quality in her wouldn't let her. "No," she gasped. She made a final frantic effort, and the wheel was on.

"Push it back as far as it'll go," he ordered.

He set the wagon down and tightened the nut with his fingers. Later he would have to put a wrench on it, but it wouldn't come off just the distance to home.

They stood there smiling at each other, knowing the mutual bond of a shared accomplishment.

"Your blouse," he said in dismay. He remembered he had put a fresh work handkerchief in his pocket that morning, and he pulled it out. He dabbed at the smears on her blouse but only succeeded in making them worse.

She caught his hand. "It doesn't matter, Oakes. Who cares?" She looked up at him, and the laughter in her eyes faded.

He could swear he hadn't the slightest intention of this, but she was in his arms without any knowledge on his part of how she got there. Her eyes had the magnetic quality of a deep, inviting pool, and he lowered his head. The hunger in her mouth startled him, then he forgot about everything else except the embrace.

He had no idea how long it lasted, but he was breathing harder when it was over. The hard rise and fall of her bosom said it had affected her the same way.

She made no effort to break the clasp of his arms about her. She leaned her weight on the circle of them, a mocking smile on her face.

"I didn't think you were human, Oakes."

"Didn't you?" His heart still pounded, and he could still taste the touch of her lips. His arms tightened, pulling her back to him.

She gave willingly, but she was unwise enough to speak of a price. "You held out longer than I expected, Oakes."

It alerted his senses, and he stared at her with a renewed clarity. He had been lost there in the sweetness of the moment, but it was gone now.

She was a vain and selfish woman, used to her own way, and unbending until she got it. She could make a prisoner of a man—if he was foolish enough to let her.

"Did I?"

She caught nothing wrong in the briefness of the answer; in fact, it only seemed to encourage her. "I knew you would have to come over to the railroad side. I knew the kind of people with the league would finally sicken you."

He could lead her on for a while, but he could see no gain to it of any kind. He didn't even want the woman. He had for a moment; he admitted it, but the moment would never return. He should end this so there could be no uncertainty in her mind, and he was trying to think of how to say it with the least hurt to her.

He couldn't put it in any way that wouldn't hurt and infuriate her, and as long as it had to be done, he might as well turn it to advantage. He saw his way to lop off another head of the snake that plagued him.

He drew a deep breath. "Will it be long before I see you again?"

Triumph made a glint in her eyes. "I'll be in town in the morning."

He made his voice sound shaky. "Can I see you there?"

Her smile deepened. "If you're man enough you can." She was aware of the talk about them.

Quincy had cleverly planted and nursed it. She would give the talk more nursing.

She leaned forward and brushed his lips with a kiss. "Until tomorrow morning, Oakes."

She climbed into the buggy before he could move to help her, then gave him a long, shining regard.

He watched the buggy until it was out of sight. "Don't fret yourself," he said aloud. "She's got a use for you. It showed in her eyes."

Saturday was always a busy day in town. She hadn't set a definite place to meet her, but the town wasn't that big that he would have trouble finding her. He wondered if at the last moment he could go through with it, for it had its elements of cruelty. He reminded himself he was only playing by her rules, and his weakness vanished.

She came riding toward him, and she made quite a picture. She saluted him with her crop, and the gesture had a carelessly assured quality.

She pulled up beside him and looked down at him, and he thought with a curious detachment, She thinks she owns me now. She no longer has to be as careful as she was. She inspected him like some prize animal, and he colored under her appraisal.

"Wait here for me," she ordered. "I must have a new dress fitted."

"Why, no, Reta. I won't wait."

She gasped at the unexpectedness of it, and an instant anger flamed in her face. "Why, I thought—"

"I know exactly what you thought. You thought a kiss would tie me up forever. I've kissed women before. Some of them much better."

He had seen evidence of her temper before. This outbreak would be monumental. Already her words had turned clipped and brittle. "Then, yesterday, why did you—"

He shrugged. "Kiss you? You helped me when I needed it. I owed you a favor."

The blood drained out of her face, leaving it pinched and white. "You conceited fool."

He watched her closely, for he expected anything of her. She leaned far out of the saddle and slashed at him with the crop, and he felt its whistling breath fan his cheek.

He jumped back, and she wheeled the horse, driving it at him. He heard a couple of startled cries from behind him and heard the pound of running feet. He had the attention of everybody on the street. He wanted to prolong this until nobody had any doubts as to the relationship between Oakes Paulson and Reta Dackett.

"You're making quite a spectacle of yourself, Reta."

She was in the grip of a terrible anger, and he doubted she even heard him. Judging by the twisted emotion of her face, he was lucky she was armed with nothing more formidable than the whip.

She slashed at him again, and he caught the force of the blow on his palm. His fingers tried to close on the whip and were too late. His palm was work-hardened, and still it stung. He certainly didn't want a cut across the face.

He made no attempt to run from her. He stayed in the middle of the street, ducking and dodging. The crowd grew, and he heard ribald comments. He thought she would have weakened by now, but her rage seemed to be feeding her strength, and maybe he would have to run before this was over. This wasn't the same immaculate woman who had ridden into this street a few minutes ago. Her blouse had pulled out of her skirt, and her hair had fallen down into her face. Her cheeks were splotched with patches of anger; and with the sun and her exertion, it wasn't impossible that she could have a stroke.

"Reta!" The voice was coldly commanding. Dackett pushed out from the crowd. His face was composed enough, but the eyes were insane with rage. "Reta!" He yelled her name with all the power of his lungs. It got through to her, and she whipped her head toward him. She stared at him, then whirled the horse, her hand lashing it at the same time. It was in full run before she cut it the second time.

Dackett stared at Oakes, and eyes could hold

no more hating. His wife had done something he would never do; she had lost her temper and with it her pride. And that hurt his pride.

"Paulson." His voice was at conversational level. "I made a bad mistake with you. And I can never rest easy unless I correct my mistakes."

Oakes spat into the dust between Dackett's feet. "You do that."

He thought for a moment he had driven the man beyond restraint. Then Dackett turned and lunged away. A hard little grin tugged at Oakes's lips. Nobody could say now there was a bond of any kind between him and the Dackett family.

Chapter Thirteen

Ross had wanted to go on the hog drive, but Oakes had turned him down. "Use your head, Ross. You can't leave Josie alone for that long a time." They had two hundred miles ahead of them, and Oakes didn't have the slightest idea of how far hogs could be driven in a day. He felt pulled at from all sides, and he felt as though things were rushing to a head. He admitted Ryan's urgency, but he wished he wasn't committed to it. A couple of days ago Ryan had said, "Oakes, I've got to drive them."

Oakes had been aware of the harried expression in Ryan's eyes and wondered if Dackett was putting the screws on him. He had nodded and said, "See how many men you can round up." This was another thing he didn't know; how many men it would take to handle the hogs. But if they erred, it had better be on the side of too many.

Ross had snapped a stick he was holding in two. "Damn it, we never do anything together anymore."

Ross couldn't stand the two hammer blows of routine and monotony, and the brief communication that had been between them when they had first moved onto their land was gone.

"We don't do anything together, Ross, because you're rarely around." Tension was drawing him through a knothole, and he was in no mood to try to reason with Ross.

"I don't know how long I'll be gone. Don't you spend a lot of time away from here." He saw the anger sweep Ross's face and didn't care. When he returned, he and Ross were coming to a definite understanding. Ross was going to pick up his half of the work and responsibility and carry them.

A dozen men were gathered at Ryan's, and they had self-conscious grins. This was something new for all of them. Ryan had the wagon packed with supplies and the temporary fencing, and there was no joking in him. The tension in him had a twanging quality, and Oakes thought Ryan wouldn't draw an easy breath until the hogs were sold.

"Let 'em out," he called, and Ryan nodded and opened the gate.

The hogs bunched up before it, eyeing this easy freedom with suspicion. Then a couple of the bolder ones scampered through it. Instantly the rest broke behind them, and men raved and swore as they chased the squealing, darting forms. As Oakes had noted before, a hog was a difficult animal to corner; it could cut in the space of a hoof print and reverse its direction, and the chase had to be taken up all over. It took an hour to hammer the initial run out of them, and the horses were panting from the effort of keeping those hogs roughly bunched, and pushed in the general direction the riders wanted them to go.

Oakes knew hogs were stubborn, ornery creatures, but he hadn't anticipated this much fight. Maybe a few miles would knock some of it out of them. He hoped so, for if they weren't ready to settle down by nightfall, the men would have a mess of trouble on their hands. Ryan's temporary fence was a clever device, wire reinforced with sticks woven through it, and it would hold weary hogs that only wanted to bed down, but it wouldn't hold hogs that had any wild left in them. A hog was a notorious fence tester, always seeking a weak spot, and this temporary fencing would go before the first concentrated seeking.

Oakes sighed as the last animal was driven into the ring formed by the temporary fencing. The two ends were wired together, and he watched anxiously as the hogs sniffed and snorted at it. But their inquisitiveness was weakened by weariness, and they started lying down.

Oakes wouldn't claim they were out of the woods yet. How long would it take the hogs to get rested enough to climb back on their feet? If they broke out at night, how would they ever be found and put back? He wished this drive was over. He grinned wryly. He had barely started, and he was yearning for the ending.

Ryan gazed out over the animals. "We'll do

better tomorrow, Oakes. It took us time to get strung out the first day."

Four men had the first guard, and Oakes watched them making their endless circles about the ring. "Will that be enough to hold them?"

"I hope so. We need sleep." Ryan's tone held worry. "I've never tried this before. I don't know what we can run into."

Oakes's eyes were sympathetic as Ryan moved away. Ryan had every right to his worry.

It was a quiet night, though Oakes got little sleep. He dozed fretfully, then something would startle him into alertness. Each time he sat up and listened, and the tension put a physical ache in him. All he heard was the muffled beats of the watch's steps and an occasional soft chuffing sound from the hogs. He would listen quite a while before the tension drained away and he could go back to sleep.

He was tired in the morning, and the same tiredness showed on the other men's faces. This kind of weariness was cumulative, each day adding its additional burden. He thought of all the days ahead of them and groaned.

It was a dull, uneventful day. The hogs tried several tentative breaks, but there was no real effort behind them. Oakes saw an indication of better times ahead. The hogs would pile up their oppressive load of weariness, and that should keep them fairly well anchored. They should be in Fresno sometime tomorrow. The drive wasn't definitely set for San Francisco. Ryan would sell anytime he got close to his price. The Orientals were scattered all through the towns strung up and down the length of California. Oakes didn't care if Ryan sold only one or a dozen. Each time he made a sale, it took that many more off of their hands.

They crowded the hogs into the temporary pen, and Ryan threw out feed for them. This second day had gone far better than the first.

Oakes came wide awake, with the feeling that he had been asleep for a good while. For a moment his thoughts groped, and he couldn't pick out what had roused him. Then he heard it, somewhat similar to the sound of distant thunder. But it couldn't be. It was too rhythmic and regular, and it never diminished. It increased steadily in volume, and Oakes saw a dark, bobbing blur moving at them hard and fast.

He jumped to his feet, uncertain which way to run. The sound was hoofbeats, and the dark blur was that of horsemen, bearing down swiftly on them.

"Raiders!" he yelled. Most of the men were on their feet, and he kicked at a couple that were slow wakening. He didn't know how many men were coming at them, or their purpose. He only knew they were right in the horsemen's path.

He saw the flash of a gun and ducked from the sound of the bullet's passage. Escape was uppermost in the men's minds, and they scattered in all directions. Oakes saw two men bowled over by horsemen, and another rider rose in his stirrups and swung a rifle stock at a running head. The man ducked and went down in a sprawl, and Oakes couldn't tell whether the stock had knocked him down or he had tripped.

The horsemen drove straight for the temporary fencing, and for a few ticks of time, the shouting of men and the squealing from the hogs was a din that battered at ears. The fence flattened, and the hogs scattered like a pile of dead leaves hit by a sudden high wind.

The actual assault was probably no longer than a dozen deep breaths. Then the raiders were gone, disappearing into the cover of the night. And Ryan's horses went with them. Oakes dropped an arm across Ryan's shoulder, knowing there was nothing anybody could do to ease this moment for him.

"They're all gone, Oakes." Ryan's voice had a ripping tear in it.

"Maybe not, Ryan. Maybe we can gather them up in the morning."

"By morning, we won't see them again. And how are we going to gather them up? The horses are scattered."

Oakes understood how Ryan was being driven,

and kept his patience. "We'll have to find the horses first, then—"

Ryan gave him a searing glance. "And that gives the hogs more time to get farther away. We've seen the last of them." He whirled and walked away.

Oakes didn't blame Ryan, but his own patience was frayed, too. He had thought of everything he could to do, and it wasn't enough. Ryan didn't blame him, but he felt no charity toward any human. It would be best for Ryan if he sat by himself until the bitterness of this weakened.

The rest of them sat and talked the remainder of the night. No man felt like sleep, and they cast worried glances toward Ryan. He sat by himself, staring at nothing, and looking carved out of stone.

"He's taking it hard," Fessler observed.

Oakes nodded. But that money wasn't the last in the world. When Ryan lifted his head up out of the gloom, they would talk about it. Oakes was sure of one thing. Dackett wasn't picking up Ryan's land because of this.

Fessler picked up a handful of sand and flung it from him. "I never even got off a shot."

Oakes grunted. Very few of them had.

"I guess we're lucky we got off with only a few bruises. Oakes, did you see masks on them?"

Oakes thought he had. He wished he could lay his hands on some of them about now.

Fessler wanted to talk more about it, but Oakes thought they would be smarter if they got some sleep. "If I'm asleep at dawn, kick me awake, Fessler. I want to get after those horses as soon as I can."

"You do the same for me. All of us want to get after them."

They walked several miles before they saw their first horse. It took most of the morning before they could coax it into standing until they could catch up with it. Each time it broke and ran in short spurts it was followed with language that should have stripped the hide off it. After that first horse was captured, picking up the others went far easier. But they never saw a hog.

They had enough of the horses caught before noon to mount most of the men. Oakes said, "I think those hogs will hit for the nearest water. We'll find the streams and scour them."

Ryan's eyes held a hard gleam. "It won't do any good, Oakes. You might find a few, but the bunch is scattered so far by now that we can never put it back together."

"But we can't just forget them, Ryan."

"I won't."

Oakes argued with him, but he made no headway. Oakes tried to reason with him until he grew angry.

"You can't take this loss, Ryan."

A strange, bleak smile moved Ryan's lips. "I don't intend to take it, Oakes. We know who was behind it. I think Dackett will make it good." He wouldn't say more. He wrapped himself in some kind of armor that Oakes couldn't penetrate.

Chapter Fourteen

Mundro laughed harshly. "You were gone only three days, Oakes. But it wasn't dull."

Oakes waited. Mundro's laugh said it wasn't going to be good news.

"It looks as though the railroad is ready to move. They sent in a land grader, and he's already at work. I tried to talk to him to get an idea of what kind of a price he's setting, but the marshal, who's always with him, chased me away. They're loading the town with outside law, Oakes. Every train seems to bring in another marshal or two."

Oakes shook his head. "Maybe I've given the league wrong advice from the beginning."

"You think you should have used violence?"

"Would we be any worse off?"

"You might be dead."

Oakes passed that over. "I can't hold them in check much longer, Galen. And whatever they do, I won't blame them. My God, man, do you realize what we face? They could throw us off of our land."

Mundro shook his head. "It's never been your land, Oakes. You haven't paid a penny on it. You've only got one course. And it might be a poor one. You've got to wait for publicity to open people's eyes. I'm filing every story I can."

"And it's doing no good."

"Not yet. You've got to remember these are local courts, courts in sympathy with the railroad, deciding against us. It takes time to go higher. Damn it, Oakes, you've got to believe there's justice somewhere. Or you might as well grab up your gun and start using it."

"That has its appeal. It wouldn't take much for me to shoot Dackett."

"He's only a sign of the times. If he was gone, the railroad would only send someone else like him to do the same kind of pushing. It'll go on until the country knows what is happening and rebels against the railroad. Little people can be powerful, too—if they band together."

"And while we're waiting for them to band together, the big interests chew us up a bite at a time."

Mundro laughed. "But enough of those little bites can give them indigestion."

Oakes blew out his breath. "I hope you know what you're talking about."

Dackett stood at the window, watching Paulson and Mundro until they separated. Those were the two who were fomenting all the trouble. If he could only get rid of them—Of course, there had been no real violence as yet, but the threat of it hung in the air. Every time he passed a group of men, his palms sweated. And Oakes Paulson could trigger that violence any time he wanted to. The railroad had set Dackett a hard job, getting this new price for the land. That grader had set some of the prices 10 to 15 times higher than the original ones on the circulars. When the news got out, this valley would explode. There was great personal danger to him. He had to whittle away a shaving at a time, or he could throw everything into open war. If the home office would quit complaining about his slowness and send in more law, they would see how fast he could move. The local law was almost useless. Henshaw was so frightened at the building tension that he was talking of resigning. Whelen never talked much, and Dackett didn't exactly know where he stood.

A moment ago he had watched two men and blamed his troubles on them. But Paulson was really the key. If he could get rid of him, Mundro would be helpless. And most of the settlers would run like frightened quail. Ryan's note was coming up in a week. But Dackett was afraid to go ahead and collect it, because of Oakes Paulson. He knew how close the two men were, but he didn't know how far Paulson's friendship would go.

He moved back to the window and stared out again. Ross Paulson and his wife were just pulling up before Bennett's store. Ross's face had a sullen set as he helped Josie from the wagon. The two brothers were worlds apart in every characteristic. Josie was a pretty thing. She didn't have Reta's flashy beauty, but she had a full-blooded warmth that Reta lacked.

A gleam started in Dackett's eyes as a new thought proposed itself. Reta had no reason to like Oakes. She might consider anything that would rip his family life to shreds. A man torn apart with that kind of emotional problem certainly wasn't going to be able to put much attention on other people's troubles. If nothing came of it, what could he lose?

He looked out the window again. Ross Paulson sat on the wagon seat, staring blankly at nothing. Dackett glanced at his watch. Usually Reta came into town every morning. This would probably be the one morning she didn't. He looked at his loaded desk and swore. Everything was being dumped on him these days.

Reta didn't like walking, even for a few blocks, but that loose shoe had to be fixed. She had ranted at that stubborn blacksmith, but she hadn't been able to sway him. He couldn't get to the loose shoe until after lunch. He was an old man, and the sardonic gleam in his eyes said she had no physical powers to move him.

She kept to the shade all she possibly could. She had seen Oakes three or four times after her effort to quirt him. They hadn't exchanged a word. Just the sight of him put her anger into full flame. But deep down, she admitted a gnawing hurt. The big, stupid ox had reached her, and she didn't know why. Was it his size and physical strength? In her reflective moments, she had asked herself several questions about him. She didn't know the answers. But she wished she could control him, even if only for a short time. She would cripple him for humiliating her.

She felt eyes on her, and she glanced toward the wagon. Ross Paulson was in it, and he beamed at her. She let her eyes touch his, and her face grew cold. He was far more handsome than his brother, but she had only contempt for him. Each time he saw her he tried to make some advantage of the contact, and she withered him. Color started in his face now at her frozen impassiveness, and it tickled her. She wished she could make Oakes squirm as easily.

She moved by the wagon. He turned his head to follow her; she could feel it.

She walked into her husband's office, and he regarded her with sardonic eyes. She hated him. At the start, she had thought she could enslave him, but he had been the stronger. How many times had she threatened to leave him, and he had only laughed? He knew she couldn't leave him. Where would she go and how would she live?

He watched her move restlessly about the office. "Will you sit down? You've been a caged animal ever since Paulson humiliated you."

Her face turned raw with passion. "He did not humiliate me. I whipped him."

He looked at her with brutal eyes. "Which one do you think people are laughing at? You never touched him, and you know it."

She ducked her head. She couldn't let him see the betraying fury in her face.

He laughed softly. "Women think with their emotions. They can only see one way to hit a target. If I was a woman and wanted to hurt Paulson, I could do it."

She must not let her eagerness show. She shrugged to show her disinterest.

"I'd hurt him through his brother. And his sister-in-law. Haven't you seen him look at her? Watch him the next time they're in town. Watch him hand her down from the wagon. You'd think he was handling eggs. But she sees only Ross. And Ross sees every woman. I'd hurt her through Ross. And Oakes would suffer because she did."

She looked at him in long, level weighing. He had a fiendish intelligence in the way he could analyze people and strike at their weakest spots. He was so right. Why hadn't she seen this before?

She stayed another five minutes, chattering about minor things, not wanting him to know he had put an idea into her head. She didn't see him smile as she closed the door, nor did she hear him murmur, "Reta, you're not really a clever woman."

The wagon was still there. Ross's back was

toward her, but at the sound of her footsteps he turned his head. He started to smile, then a sullen stiffness seized his face.

She gave him a tentative little smile, and his face brightened with hope. She slowed her pace and let the smile grow. He beamed all over his face. What a fatuous fool he was.

As she moved by his wagon she turned her head toward him, then jerked it forward as though determined she would not let her interest show. She stumbled and lost her balance, going to one knee before she caught herself. Her gasped "Oh" was loud enough to carry to him.

She heard the thud as his feet hit the ground. She hadn't thought it possible a man could move so fast. His hands went under her elbows, helping her to her feet. "Are you hurt?"

She took a tentative step and winced. "I may have turned my ankle."

"Oh no," he breathed.

He threw a guilty glance toward the store, and she knew his dilemma. He didn't want to leave her, and at the same time, he didn't want his wife to step out and see them.

"If you could help me to my husband's office—" She leaned her weight on him. "I would be in your debt."

He looked at the store entrance again. A little, frightened man. But he could be the tool through which she hurt Oakes Paulson.

He took a deep, trembling breath. "Why, Mrs. Dackett, I'd like nothing better."

She gave him the full force of her eyes. He was already helpless.

Josie's eyes were numb with hurt. Oakes had tried to talk to her about it, and she had turned away. He didn't have to hear her talk to know what was wrong. And he could almost pick the exact time it had started. Some six days ago, he thought. Maybe a day more or less. But he had seen Ross's enthrallment grow progressively worse. Oakes guessed he wasn't very bright. He'd had to see Reta and Ross together in town yesterday for him to realize fully what was happening. Anybody but a blind man could see it. Ross had that stupid look as Reta laughed up into his face. It couldn't have been plainer if both of them had shouted it at Oakes.

Josie stood off by herself again, and she didn't realize he was watching her. That special kind of anguish molded her face again. He didn't care how much she rebuffed him; he was going to have this out with her. He didn't know what it was going to be, but he was going to do something about this, even if it had to include knocking Ross's head off.

He strode to her and seized her wrist. "Don't duck me, Josie. Ross wasn't home last night or the night before."

She tried to meet his eyes, and she couldn't.

The defiance in her face had no solid basis. "He might have come in late, Oakes. I don't know. I was asleep."

He scowled at her. "Don't lie to me, Josie. And he's going out tonight, isn't he?"

Wildness was in her voice. "I don't know. Leave me alone." She broke free and whirled from him.

He had handled that clumsily, but he had a final answer. She knew. His hands ached with the desire to close on Ross. He heard whistling coming from the well, and he strode toward it. Josie probably wouldn't appreciate this, but he had to say something to Ross.

Ross had finished his bath and was dressing. Drops of water still sparkled on his shoulders. Oakes surveyed him silently a moment. He was a handsome man. It was surprising he hadn't caught Reta Dackett's eye before now.

Ross smiled. He looked like a happy man, and Oakes thought grimly, He won't be by the time I finish.

"Are you going into town again tonight?"

Ross made a deprecatory gesture. "You know how it is."

"No, I don't. Tell me."

Ross's smile turned into a frown. "Business, Oakes. A man has to take care of it no matter what demands it makes on him."

Oakes's wrath had reached the boiling point.

"Why, you damned liar! Who do you think you're fooling? That Dackett woman has turned you into a complete idiot."

Ross breathed hard. "Stay out of my business, Oakes."

"Not when it affects me. And Josie. Don't you care what you're doing to her?"

"I'll let you worry about that."

Oakes's fists clenched. "What are you trying to say?"

He had never heard a nastier laugh. "And who are you trying to fool? I've watched that sick-calf look on your face when you look at her. Don't try to pour any righteous anger on me. How do I know what's been happening between you two? You've had the opportunity—"

Oakes chopped off the words with a hard fist against the jaw. He didn't spare anything, and Ross flew back a couple of steps, his arms flying up for balance. But any action he took was only reflex, for his eyes were glassy and rolling up into his head. His knees broke on him and he spilled to the ground, sprawling on his back.

Oakes stood over him, breathing hard. He didn't have the slightest regret. He wished Ross was still on his feet. He would like to swing at him again. He drew a bucket of water. The bruise on Ross's chin was beginning to show up nicely. He doused the water into Ross's face. Ross spluttered, then opened his eyes and stared stupidly about.

Oakes watched him with bleak eyes. He had better get out of here. It was too much temptation to stand Ross on his feet and knock him down again.

He hoed in the garden, and his blind anger made him do more damage than good. He heard the furious pound of hooves and didn't raise his head. He chopped at weeds and vegetables alike until he was dripping sweat. Only Josie's voice raised his head.

"Oakes, what did you say to him?"

"Nothing, Josie."

"The way he tore out of here you had to say something."

He couldn't stand her accusing eyes. Why did the worthless men get the best women? "I hit him."

Her eyes widened, and he spoke out of a mixture of anger and self-defense. "He earned it, several times over. He said some ugly things about—" He saw how he had trapped himself. He couldn't tell her of Ross's accusation, or she would never be able to spend another comfortable moment around him.

"Nothing," he mumbled. "It wasn't anything at all, Josie. I lost my head and made something out of nothing at all."

He didn't look at her, but he could feel her eyes on him.

"Was it your fault, Oakes?" Her voice seemed

infinitely weary. "You would be better off if you stayed out of our affairs."

He didn't blame her for the bitterness he knew she felt. He apologized and tried to explain at the same time, and she shook her head. He thought there had to be a big streak of charity in her, for she tried to take some of the load off his back.

"Forget it, Oakes. He will be back. He always has before."

He stared at her with puzzled eyes. Had that been indifference in her last remark?

Chapter Fifteen

Oakes's face was set hard as he rode into town the following morning. He wasn't sure what he was going to do, but he had to do something. At breakfast, his heart had ached at the sight of Josie's face. There was so much hurt behind those remote eyes. She wasn't angry at him or unkind; her mind was too filled with other things to be much more than merely aware of him. Neither of them ate very much.

He shouldn't have interfered; he could see plainly now where he had only made it worse. Ross had a vindictive streak. He would punish both of them by staying away longer than he ordinarily would have. Oakes might be able to change Ross's mind. He had no doubt it came under meddling again, but he had to make one more effort.

If he found Ross, could he control his temper? That was an interesting question, unanswerable until he saw him.

He drove into town and searched the likely haunts. Ross wasn't in any of the saloons or card games. He really didn't expect to find him there. Ross was with Reta, and that made a long list of places he might be. He saw Wiley watching him with that fixed snake stare, and it didn't ruffle him. He had never heard of a stare leaving any permanent scars.

Mundro caught him at a corner. "Oakes, I've just learned something. The railroad's selling land to men who are willing to pay the price."

Oakes frowned at him. "I didn't know there was any empty land left."

Mundro's face was grim. "There isn't. The railroad's selling occupied land. They're selling to men who have just come in. They'll want their land, and you know whose side they'll be on."

Oakes was still trying to puzzle this through. "Somebody will have to be evicted before somebody else can take possession?"

"That's it exactly."

"The railroad wouldn't be that crazy. Every time they tried to evict a man, they would need a half-hundred lawmen to protect the one who was serving the papers."

"Maybe they know that. A half-dozen men got off the train yesterday. They had the stamp of lawmen on them. Add those to what's already here—Oakes, are you even listening to me?"

"I heard you. Tell me what to do about it, and I'll listen harder. But right now I've got something else on my mind."

He crossed the street, leaving Mundro staring after him. Ross wasn't anywhere in town, at least not anywhere he could be seen openly. But there was a hobble Oakes might put on him. He could make sure Dackett knew what was going on. Of course, an outraged husband might come shooting at Ross, but somehow Oakes doubted it.

He walked inside the railroad office, and the clerk took one look at his face and stepped aside. He threw open Dackett's door without knocking, and the surprise hadn't had time to set on Dackett's face before Oakes demanded, "Where's Ross?"

"How would I know?"

Oakes felt the tightness closing in on his throat. Anger always did that to him. "What would you say if I told you he's been seeing your wife?"

Dackett's eyes were bright with interest, but there was no outrage in them. "Why, then I'd say it looks as though I'd lost out."

Oakes's jaw sagged. He hadn't expected this. "You don't give a damn?"

It delighted Dackett to see the ground cut from under the big man's feet. "Not in the slightest."

Oakes moved around the corner of the desk. "You're going to tell him to stay away from her or you'll beat his head off. Or have it beaten off." Either threat would send Ross running.

Dackett threw back his head and roared with laughter. "Why, you damned fool. Didn't you understand me? I don't care."

Oakes grabbed him suddenly and jerked him out of his chair. He hauled him close to his face. "But you care now. You've suddenly learned you do. Send her out of town. I don't care how you handle it, but keep her away from him." He slammed Dackett back into his chair with a force that threatened to tip it over. "You wouldn't want me to come back and tell you the second time, would you?"

Dackett ran a finger around his neck where his collar had cut into it. His eyes were murderous. "No. That won't be necessary."

The fury remained on his face long after Oakes had left the room. It was time to cut Wiley loose. Oakes Paulson had been a nuisance long enough.

Josie wouldn't listen to Oakes. "We have to shop, don't we? No, you can't do it all. A few things I have to do myself."

He didn't know how much truth and how much pride were in her words. It couldn't help but hurt to go into town, and she insisted upon going anyway. Ross hadn't been home since Oakes had knocked him unconscious, and Oakes thought it was about time to see Dackett again. If Dackett hadn't taken his warning seriously the last time, he would this one.

Sure, Josie had her pride. She wasn't going to stay away from town and increase the talk, but she was still vulnerable. She didn't want to see any more people than she had to, for Oakes noticed how she found one task after another until it was almost dark before they started. It would be quite dark by the time they reached there. She wanted it that way. He knew her head would be high, but it wouldn't be as bad as walking down the street in broad daylight.

Neither of them made much pretense at talking. At the edge of town she did say, "Wasn't that Wiley?"

He whipped his head toward the narrow, dark mouth of an alley. "I didn't see him."

She shrugged, and he thought, How far apart we've grown when we have to manufacture talk.

He pulled up before Bennett's store, noticing how light the traffic was this evening. He started to step down, and Fessler came down the street. Fessler wanted to ask the same question that was on everybody's lips—what were they going to do?—and Oakes didn't know.

Fessler walked with Oakes to the hitchrack, talked while he made his wrap, and came back with him. He never missed a word, even though Oakes kept shaking his head.

Oakes reached up to hand Josie down, and Fessler said, "I tell you, Oakes, we're not going to take this lying down."

Fessler was in a nasty and unstable mood, and Oakes didn't want an argument in front of Josie. He pushed Josie ahead of him. "I'll talk to you later about it, Fessler."

Fessler stopped, and Oakes thought he was rid of him. He moved on a few steps, and Fessler called to him. Oakes sighed and turned back to him. Josie, seeing his predicament, retraced her steps to pull him out of this. He felt a strong surge of gratitude. She wasn't so wrapped up in her troubles as to be unable to see the small one he had here.

She stretched her hand toward him and opened her mouth to say something. The words didn't come. The sharp, spiteful crack of a rifle whipped back and forth across the street, and Josie cried out and staggered back. Her hand went to her upper left arm, and her face washed with shock.

That had been close, so close that Oakes had felt the wind of the bullet. He saw Josie sway and thought she was going to fall. He sprang forward, getting his body between her and the ambusher. She tried to give him a twisted smile. "I think— it's my arm, Oakes."

A stain spread on the sleeve of her dress, and the blood dripped from her elbow. Oakes still shielded her, but he thought, If there was going to be another shot, it would have come before now. A man came out of the store and blocked his way, and Oakes roared at him. "Get out of my way."

He swept her up into his arms and plodded toward the door, and every step of the way his flesh was tight in anticipation of a bullet plowing into his back. He carried her inside and sat her down on a chair. How white her face was!

"I'm all right," she kept insisting, and he was afraid she would faint at any moment.

Fessler pressed in, still not completely aware of what had happened. "What is it, Oakes?" His tone sounded querulous.

"Somebody shot at us from across the street." Oakes ripped the dress sleeve from elbow to shoulder, then let out a carefully held breath. The bleeding and the rawness of the wound made it look uglier than it really was. He snatched up a handkerchief from a pile of them on a table and pressed it against the wound. He soaked up most of the blood, and the pressure momentarily stopped the rest. Before it started again, he saw the furrow. He thought there was no bone damage, and he hoped the slug hadn't touched a muscle. Stopping the bleeding was the chief problem at the moment, and he yelled, "Get Zeller."

People were coming in off the street, and they began to cluster thickly about her.

"Goddamn it. Give her room. And somebody get the doctor."

He kept the handkerchief pressed tight against the arm until Zeller came. Zeller was a humorless, bald-headed man with an expressionless face. Watching him, a man could never tell how a sickness or hurt was going. He talked to himself in fragments of words and meaningless clucks. When he finished the bandaging, he looked up at Oakes. "Just a little worse than a nick. It will cause her some discomfort for a week. Less the following one." He had kept Oakes shifting from one foot to another, and now he grinned frostily as though he had enjoyed keeping him on the needle point of anxiety.

"Should she go home?"

Zeller shrugged. "She could make it. She probably would not enjoy it."

Lola Bennett pushed forward. She was a woman of ample proportions and a determined air. "She stays here." She rushed on over Josie's protests. "Don't you think it will be a pleasure to have somebody here who talks about something other than what happens in the store? I get so sick of listening to Jabez." She patted Josie's shoulder. "Please."

Oakes sighed with relief as he saw Josie's face give in. He took Jabez's arm and pulled the storekeeper off to one side. "Jabez, put a gun on my account."

Jabez had solemn sheep-dog eyes and a mouth that could break into an easy smile. "You think you know who shot her?"

"I might. I don't want her knowing where I'm going."

Jabez nodded. "Might be best if nobody knew. It doesn't have to be a new gun?"

Oakes shook his head.

"Come through the back rooms, then. I've got an old gun that holds true."

He shut the door behind them. "If Josie knew what you were up to, you'd get a holler."

"Yes." Oakes tried the gun's balance. It felt good to him. He was no hell with a handgun. He could hit a barn, if it held still long enough.

Jabez opened the rear door for him. "Henshaw will eventually get around to coming here. Anything you want me to tell him?"

Oakes gave him a bleak grin. "How about, go to hell, to start out with?"

Jabez nodded. "I'm in favor of it." His face sobered. "You know what you're doing, Oakes? Whoever it was, wasn't playing games."

"I think I do."

"Good luck, then."

Oakes stood outside the closed door a long moment. He thought he could go around the building, cross the street, and find the exact spot from which the ambusher had fired. He couldn't see that it would do him any particular good. He had a man in mind, and if he was wrong, he could back away with no great harm being done. Thinking back on it, it seemed to him that the last half-dozen times he had been in town Wiley was always somewhere in the background. If Wiley had fired the shot that hit Josie, Oakes thought he would show some sign of it. But Wiley was an accomplished poker player. It might stand him to good purpose in hiding this, too.

He walked into Wiley's poker game and found

five men sitting at the table with him. Wiley's eyes never flickered at Oakes's entrance, but Oakes had the hard-hitting impression that Wiley walked a razor's edge, waiting to see which direction Oakes intended carrying this. He made no attempt to conceal the pistol in his waistband. He wanted Wiley to know he carried it.

He stopped across the table from Wiley and stared at him. Wiley raised his eyes once, then dropped them hastily. But his hands never wavered, and his face was like stone.

But there was nervousness among the other men. Their eyes kept picking up Oakes, then sliding away from him.

Oakes let time push hard against nerves. Something was here among them to bother them this much.

Finally Wiley raised his head. "What the hell do you want?"

Oakes let more time drag before he answered. "There was a shooting in town tonight."

Some brief spark blazed in Wiley's eyes. It could have been the thought of a triumph of sorts. "I've been here all evening. Ask them."

Oakes got nods from the faces. He stared at Wiley. "This was particularly bad. He killed a woman."

A nerve jumped in Wiley's cheek, and his jaw sagged. For an instant it looked as though he was incapable of making a sound.

"Christ!" one of the players muttered. "The town won't stand for that. I'm not getting tied—"

"Shut up!" Wiley screamed. "You keep your goddamned mouth shut."

A new tenseness molded Oakes's face. "You don't know anything about it, Wiley?"

"I said so, didn't I?"

Oakes's nod was almost pleasant. "Then you won't object to me checking your rifle. It won't be hard to tell if it's been fired tonight. It's in your room, isn't it? Don't get up. I know where it is."

He turned and took several steps. He heard the scrape of a chair and a hoarse yell. He tugged the pistol clear as he whirled. Wiley was on his feet, the size of his hand dwarfing the gun it held. His mouth was a bared slash in a maniacal face as he leveled the weapon at Oakes. The derringer made its coughing grunt, and Oakes felt something slam him in the arm. It brought no great pain, or even shock. He leveled his pistol at the slash of Wiley's mouth and pulled the trigger.

Wiley managed to get his hands up to his face before he fell. Blood was spurting through his fingers before he hit the floor.

Shock held the room silent and motionless, then an awed voice said, "Jesus."

Oakes looked from face to face. He held the pistol partially raised. It pointed at no particular man, and yet every man could swear it pointed directly at him. His eyes clubbed each face in turn. "Did anybody see this differently than it happened?"

He received an emphatic denial from every shaking head. One of them said, "He just sort of seemed to go crazy."

Oakes nodded gravely. "It looked that way to me, too. Henshaw will want to know how it was. I guess we'd all better wait until he gets here."

He felt something trickling down his arm and looked at his hand in surprise. That was blood running down it. He would be damned if Wiley hadn't pinked him.

He took off his coat and examined his left arm. Wiley had gotten him through the underneath side. It was bleeding freely, and it had started hurting. A thought struck him, and he almost grinned. He could match Josie now.

He pulled out a handkerchief, and one of the men helped him tie it into place. Not that he needed it, but he had one more question he wanted to ask.

"Wiley was out this evening, wasn't he?"

Eyes turned furtive until one of the men said, "What difference does it make now? He told us to say he was here all evening. But he wasn't."

Oakes nodded. "I kind of thought so."

Henshaw came in a few moments afterward. He looked at Wiley, and something painted a pallor on his face. "What the hell happened?"

Five voices tried to talk at once. The gist of the babble was that Wiley had practically tried to commit suicide. He had shot Oakes with that little pea gun while Oakes's back was turned. Oakes had used a bigger gun, and his aim had been better.

Oakes watched Henshaw with bright eyes. That arm was sure raising hell. "Well, Sheriff?"

The pallor remained in Henshaw's face, and confusion made his voice uncertain. "I guess it happened the way they say. But I still can't understand—"

"Maybe somebody besides Wiley doesn't like me."

Henshaw gave him a suspicious glance. "What's that mean?"

"I was just thinking somebody else could wind up like Wiley." Oakes could hear Henshaw's spluttering as he walked out the door.

Mundro was hurrying down the street, and he grabbed for Oakes's arm. Oakes jerked the left one out of the way. "That one's kind of sensitive."

"What happened?"

"Wiley and I just disagreed. He shot me with that little popgun he carries." He shook his head at the concern in Mundro's face. "It's just a scratch. I'll let Zeller look at it."

"I just came from Bennett's store. Did Wiley shoot Josie?"

"There's no doubt of it."

Mundro's eyes picked up the pistol in the waistband. "And you killed Wiley. You came here with only that purpose."

Oakes bristled. Mundro sounded as though he blamed him for what had had to be done. "I told you there was no doubt—"

Mundro made an impatient gesture. "I'm wasting no grief on him. But it's too bad he's dead. He might have talked about who hired him to lay that ambush."

Oakes gave that slow thought, then shook his head. "He had enough reason. I had trouble with him when I first came here."

"Then why did he wait until now? No, I think somebody held him in check until now."

"Dackett?" Oakes sounded startled. "I did have a recent run-in with him."

"Hah!" Mundro pointed a finger. "Doesn't it all fit?"

Oakes admitted that it could. And he could see why Mundro thought that it was too bad that Wiley was dead. But even if Wiley had named Dackett, would it be enough to pull Dackett down?

Mundro pounded his fist into his palm. "Just once I'd like to have something solid to move against Dackett with. We're handicapped fighting him."

"Why?" Oakes didn't really have a great deal of interest in the answer. He was more interested in getting something to ease the pound in his arm.

"Because we try to use lawful steps, and it isn't enough."

Oakes raised his arm and looked at it. The bleeding had soaked through the handkerchief and was beginning a steady dripping.

Mundro saw it, too. "We've got to get you to Zeller." He laughed, and Oakes's face turned sour at the sound.

"I'm glad somebody is enjoying it."

"Not that, Oakes. I couldn't help thinking that between you and Josie, you're giving Zeller a busy evening."

Chapter Sixteen

The sling hardly hampered Oakes at all. He probably could discard it before he picked up Josie. He hoped the two days had given her a rest and a change.

He lifted the reins and looked down at Ryan. "You sure you don't want a ride in?" He was worried about Ryan. The man hadn't been the same since the day he lost his hogs. He had such an unreal, faraway look, and he never seemed to be listening whenever anybody talked to him. "Ryan, did you hear me?"

Ryan lifted his head with a start. "I heard you. I might ride in later on in the day, Oakes." That strange, secretive smile touched his face. "Do you know what tomorrow is?"

The day had no special significance to Oakes. But then, he had been pretty well occupied with a multitude of problems. "No, what is it?"

"My note's due with Dackett."

Oakes had tried to talk to Ryan about it before and had gotten nowhere. Ryan had more than made it plain that he looked for no help from anybody. But why did he bring it up at this late minute?

"Ryan, I've told you, I can let you have the money."

Ryan shook his head. "If I can't take care of it, Oakes, I'll let you know."

Oakes looked back after a dozen yards. That odd smile was still on Ryan's face. Now wasn't that the damnedest thing, the way that all came about? Oakes shook his head in worry. Ryan just wasn't the same anymore.

He took off the sling before he stopped in front of Bennett's store. He moved the arm experimentally. If he got reckless with it, it was going to twinge on him, but he didn't see any reason to say anything at all about it to Josie.

Josie kissed and hugged Lola Bennett at the door, then squeezed Jabez's hand. "You are two of the dearest people I know. I won't even try to say thank you."

Lola Bennett sighed. "If you knew how bad I hate to see you leave. Now I have to go back to talking to Jabez."

Josie's laugh rang out, and Jabez grinned. Oakes didn't have Jabez's pistol with him, and he said, "Jabez, I forgot your gun."

Jabez waved a hand in dismissal. "Keep it. You might need it again."

Josie laughed at Oakes's solicitous care in helping her into the wagon. "I'm not an egg, Oakes. How's your arm?" She tried to look severe at his guilty look. "Didn't you think I would hear about it?"

"I hoped you wouldn't. I didn't want you worrying about any part of it."

"You did what you had to do, didn't you? I don't want either of us to think about it."

His face cleared. His next question was ticklish, but he had to know. "Did Ross come to see you?"

She stared straight ahead, and for a long moment he thought she would make no reply. Slowly, she shook her head. "He didn't. Didn't he come out to the house?"

She could read the answer in his face. He hurt so badly for her, and there wasn't a thing he could do. He wished he could find Ross right now. One hand was all he needed to beat his head off.

She didn't speak another word the rest of the way home, and he didn't try to batter down her defenses.

He helped her down. "Don't worry about supper, Josie. I'll take care of it."

She gave him an indignant glance. "I'm not helpless."

He worked savagely until suppertime. Maybe she didn't know it, but they were both helpless.

He smoked for a long time after it was dark. He had come to this land fearing and hating it, and it had turned a smiling face toward him. Now he had the feeling that face was beginning to turn away. He saw the light in the house go out. His best hadn't been able to hold this family together. He listened to the night sounds, and they should have brought peace. But how could he know peace when he looked into a trackless void?

He sucked on the pipe until he pulled its sour juices into his mouth. He spat in quick distaste, rubbed his tongue with the back of his hand, and stood. How long he had sat here he didn't know, but he could tell by the wheel of the stars that it was getting late. He rolled his shoulders to ease them. He knew the bone-driven weariness that rest couldn't ease.

He jerked his head around as he heard the quick, hard pound of hooves. That kind of sound always carried its urgency, particularly this late at night.

He moved toward the road, knowing this might not be for him at all.

"Oakes! Oakes!"

He sighed as the call removed any doubt. He wasn't to the road yet, and he waved his arm to catch the rider's attention.

The man cut off the road and headed toward him, throwing his words ahead of him. "Oakes, it's Ryan."

Oakes recognized Fessler's voice, and premonition sank icy claws into him. He hurried forward until Fessler hauled in the horse. Oakes took its bridle. "Has he been hurt?" Fessler's tone only went with bad news.

"Worse. He's been shot. He tried to hold up the railroad office."

Oakes heard every word; still he couldn't sort and put them in their proper place. He groaned hollowly. Now he understood some of the crazy, veiled references Ryan had made. Ryan had brooded too long over his loss, and he had hit directly at the man he thought responsible.

"He was hit as he came out of the office, Oakes. He lost his mask then. A lot of people saw him. There's no doubt."

"Is he dead?" It was hard to ask that.

"They didn't even capture him. Zeller saw the spot where he fell. He said it wasn't possible that a man could ride after losing that much blood, but Ryan got out of town."

"Do you know where he headed?"

"I'm ahead of the posse. I was hoping you had seen him."

Oakes's thoughts darted frantically about, like mice flushed out of the safety of their hole. Where would Ryan go, where could he begin to look for him?

"Fessler, can I take your horse?"

Fessler was already sliding out of the saddle. "Thought you'd want it. You're looking at his house first? Good. I'll stay here and see if I can delay the posse."

Oakes pressed his shoulder before he swung into the saddle. He put the horse into a full run and never looked back.

Ryan's place looked as though nobody was

home, but it didn't have that alone feeling. His horse wasn't in the shed, and still it seemed wrong to Oakes. If Ryan was as hard hit as Fessler said, he had to have some kind of help, even if it was self-administered at home.

He stood in the middle of the shed and yelled again. The mocking echoes made him want to rave. "Goddamn it, Ryan. I know you're here. Answer me."

He started as the lid to a feed bin slowly raised. He caught the glint of a rifle barrel and yelled, "Ryan! It's me. Oakes."

Ryan pushed the lid all the way back with the barrel. "I know who it is. Did you think I was going to shoot you?" That sounded like the whisper of a dry chuckle in his voice.

Oakes leaped to him and helped him out of the bin. He had to take most of Ryan's weight, and he saw the sweat start on his forehead. He didn't have to ask how bad it was. The blood-soaked pant leg told him that. The wound was in a bad place, high in the thigh almost in the juncture of leg and trunk, and it was difficult to put and keep a tourniquet on it. The exertion started new bleeding, and Oakes saw the fresh glisten of it on Ryan's pant leg.

It sounded as though Ryan forced his voice. "I had to quit riding, Oakes. I couldn't keep the bleeding stopped."

"You can't stay here. Henshaw's got a posse

after you." Oakes wished he knew where that posse was; he wished he knew how much margin he had.

Ryan's teeth bared in a mirthless grin. He raised his left hand, and for the first time Oakes noticed he held a sack in it. It wasn't difficult to guess at what it held.

"I'd have beaten them, if it hadn't been for a lucky shot."

"It was a damned fool thing to do, Ryan—You knew they'd be after you."

Ryan's face looked dangerous. "It was my money. I was entitled to it. Didn't Dackett take it from me?"

Ryan had lost a lot of blood, and he might be out of his head. Anyway, it would do no good to point out that he hadn't taken Dackett's money, that he had stolen the railroad's money. Oakes felt a heavy sense of inevitability rushing at him, a feeling that no matter how hard he tried he couldn't change or turn the course of things.

"You'll have to ride again, Ryan. The posse is on its way. Can you hold on here while I run into the house?"

Ryan nodded. "You might bring back that bottle of whiskey in the cupboard."

Oakes ran toward the house. That bleeding never let up its steady dripping. He had to get something big, like a sheet or a blanket, and maybe he could cover enough surface so that he could get sufficient pressure to at least slow the bleeding. His horse would have to carry double, but not for long because Ryan wouldn't be able to stand it. Oakes's breathing felt tight and painful. Ryan had to have a doctor's care.

He found the whiskey bottle and tucked it into a pocket. There were no sheets on the bed, and he jerked a blanket off it. As he ran back he started figuring how he could tie the blanket to bring pressure on the wound.

The mental struggle getting Ryan onto the horse was far harder than the physical. Ryan gave him a ghastly grin. He had tucked the money sack into his shirt, and he held onto his rifle despite Oakes's attempt to take it from him.

"I'm all right," he insisted.

He wasn't. His face was a twisted mask, and already the bleeding was coming through the blanket. The horse didn't like it, and Oakes had to keep jerking at its bridle to keep it from shying. Everything was closing in on him at once, and he wanted to yell under the pressure. He forced the horse quiet again and climbed up on it.

He looked around before he started the horse. The night looked so peaceful under the full moonlight. It wasn't. It boiled and seethed with violence.

Their progress was slow and painful. Oakes stopped a dozen times to check and tighten the blanket. The last time he did it, Ryan made garbled sounds that weren't words. His face looked waxy in the moonlight. Oakes had slowed the bleeding, but he hadn't entirely stopped it. He knew that Ryan was slowly bleeding to death. He realized two things: he had to get Ryan off the moving horse, and he had to get competent medical help. He had headed toward town when he first started, making only the necessary swing to avoid the posse, and he had hoped to take Ryan all the way in. Now he knew it couldn't be done that way. He would have to leave Ryan some place and bring Zeller back as fast as he could.

He saw a spot among the roots of a live oak tree that might do. It looked as though it might have started as the burrow of a wild animal, then been enlarged by erosion. It was large enough to hold Ryan, and it gave him partial shelter and concealment. Oakes would have wanted something better, but he had little choice.

The bleeding was worse by the time he got Ryan off the horse and into the hollow. Oakes got it almost stopped again. Now everything was grinding him cruelly. He needed this time to get Zeller, but he couldn't leave Ryan.

Ryan opened his eyes, and his mumbling stopped. "Oakes." His voice was clear though weak.

Oakes pressed his shoulder in response.

"I need a doctor bad, don't I?"

Oakes nodded.

"Then go on and get him. I'll be all right." Ryan's hand fumbled around beside him, and Oakes guessed what he wanted. He placed the rifle within Ryan's grasp.

"I'll hurry, Ryan."

Ryan gave him a weak, pallid grin. "I know that. And Oakes—" He hesitated a long moment. "Thanks for everything."

Oakes's face was fierce. "You know better than that. I'll be back before you know it."

Ryan still looked at him, but he didn't seem to know him now. Oakes turned and ran for the horse. Goddamn things that tripped up little people, things they were seemingly helpless to prevent happening. Damn them, damn them, damn them.

Dackett fumed in a fever of impatience. That fool of a sheriff hemmed and hawed over everything. Now he was pawing around Ryan's grain bin. Who did he think he was impressing? Anybody could see that a bleeding man had been in the bin, and that he had bled a great deal more just outside of it. Somebody had helped Ryan at this spot. Dackett hoped it was Paulson and that they could catch the two together. That would give him all the excuse he needed to see that both of them never returned to town.

He looked at Bill Whelen, and Whelen shook his head. The man knew Henshaw's picky ways.

The three railroad men didn't look too happy, and they handled their rifles awkwardly.

A suspicion crossed Dackett's mind; was Henshaw delaying because he didn't want to catch up with the wounded man?

He shifted irritably in his saddle. "Henshaw, nobody's here. We've looked through the house. If you keep fooling around, he'll have time to get down into Mexico."

Henshaw looked injured. "Too much haste could make us lose the trail."

Dackett snorted. "We won't be spending too much haste."

Whelen was good at tracking, though Dackett fretted at its slowness. Several times Whelen had to retrace his steps until he picked up another blurred track. Twice he found a dark spot of blood that looked black in the moonlight.

"How many horses?" Dackett asked.

"I'd say only one," Whelen muttered. "But by the depth of the prints in the sand, I'd say it was carrying double. But I don't understand the tracks heading toward town."

"Somebody could be trying to get Ryan to a doctor."

Whelen looked at him in admiration. "Say, that's probably it."

Dackett's irritation mounted. He had to spend his time working with fools.

He thought it was taking forever, that they were

never going to catch up with the horse before them. Then Whelen shouted.

"There's something at the base of that tree ahead. See it?" He stood in his stirrups, trying to point it out to Dackett.

Dackett couldn't see anything but a darker patch of shadow. Then there was movement in that shadow; if he used his imagination enough, he could believe a figure was trying to rise.

"Scatter," Henshaw bellowed. "He's armed and dangerous."

Henshaw and the railroad workers scattered. Dackett curbed his impulse to follow suit. Whelen stood solid, peering ahead at the tree.

"Something don't look right about that," he muttered, and moved slowly forward.

Dackett reluctantly followed. He admitted Whelen had courage.

"Hell, it's a man trying to get up," the deputy called.

Dackett could see it plainly now. The man would partially rise, then fall back. Sounds came from him that might have been broken words.

"He's raving," Whelen said. "That leg won't support him."

Dackett's face filled with hard satisfaction. It was Ryan, and he was alone.

"Ryan," he yelled. "Surrender. You're surrounded."

His voice pulled Ryan's attention, and he struggled to twist his body around. Dackett caught the glint of moonlight on metal. "Look out, Whelen. He's got a rifle."

He threw up his rifle to his shoulder and pressed the trigger. He saw Ryan jerk under the impact, and he poured in three more shots as fast as he could work the lever. Only on the last shot did Ryan sag completely to the ground.

"Goddamn it!" Whelen screamed in furious horror. "He was outa his head. He didn't know what he was doing. That rifle wasn't aimed. He was just holding it in his hand."

Dackett stared coldly at him. "I wasn't risking any of our lives on a thief."

He swung down and moved boldly to where Ryan lay. Henshaw and the others were converging on the spot. Only Whelen stayed back. Dackett knew a sudden fury toward him. He looked down, then shifted his eyes hastily from Ryan's face. That bulge in the dead man's shirt front looked unnatural, and Dackett stooped and undid a button.

He pulled out the sack, opened it enough to see the contents, and an exultant look washed his face. It was the money Ryan had taken in the holdup. Recovering it would make things so much easier. He wouldn't even have to notify the San Francisco office of the robbery. If possible, it was always best to avoid any such stories. The home office didn't take kindly to explanations that involved even the temporary loss of its money.

Chapter Seventeen

Four days weren't enough to take the pain-filled shadows out of a man's eyes. Oakes slashed at his boot with a stick, then broke it between his hands. "I'm going to kill Dackett, Galen. He riddled Ryan when it wasn't necessary. I talked to Bill Whelen. He says Ryan wasn't trying to resist or escape. He doubts Ryan even saw them. Dackett didn't call any warning to him. He just took his opportunity to kill him."

Mundro sighed. They had been over this a half-dozen times and always came to the same impasse. "I grant that everything you say is probably true, Oakes. But Ryan was a wanted man. He was armed, and it could have looked as though he was putting up a fight. Legally, Dackett had every right to do what he did. Get that crazy notion of going after him out of your head. Or you'll be on the same side of the law Ryan was."

"Can he get away with anything he wants to?"

Mundro sighed. He sympathized with Oakes, but that wasn't going to do any good. "It looks like it. But he's getting more and more and more flagrant. The law doesn't stay blind forever. He'll overstep himself one of these days."

Oakes snarled at him, "Ryan is dead."

Mundro's voice was infinitely weary. "And I still tell you not to put one foot outside the law. Not if you want to win this fight. The first violence from the settlers, and you've lost it. The railroad will move in all the law and courts it can get in the state. Oakes, give me a little more time. I've got journalists coming out from the East to see how bad this is. I've wired all the senators, and I think some of them will come out to see for themselves. If I can get what's actually happening before the public, I'll make that railroad run like a cur dog."

Oakes stared at him a long, bitter minute, then his face loosened. "I guess I can go a little longer."

Mundro rested his hand on his shoulder. "Then will you come and talk the hotheads into waiting with you? Halderman has them stirred up so much they're almost ready to slop over into the fire."

Behind him, Oakes heard Josie's movements in the house. A man's decisions rarely affected only himself. They reached out and touched so many others. A brief rebellion flared in him at the road he was being pushed along. A man was crazy if he thought he dictated his own actions. Events and circumstances dictated them for him.

He scowled at Mundro. "Let's go. Damned if you're not worse than a conscience."

Dackett looked at the figures with satisfaction. This could be the start of the collapse of the

Settlers' League. Four of the original settlers had come in and bought their land yesterday, paying the new and much higher price without too much protest. The strain had been too much for them, and they could stand it no longer. Dackett had told them that outside people were clamoring to buy the land at any price, and only the bigness of his heart was holding it for the men who first filed on it. But he couldn't hold it forever. Soon it was going to be sold to anybody who offered the right price for it.

He trimmed a cigar and lit it. He had handled that well, for the story would spread, and other men would wonder if they were doing the right thing by waiting, would wonder until they could stand it no longer.

For a while, he had been afraid Paulson and Ryan might be a strong rallying point that could beat him, but it wasn't going to happen. Ryan was dead, and Paulson seemed vague and uncertain. If he could only get rid of Paulson, the last resistance would crumble. How was the best way to do it? Why, simply throw Paulson off his land. He smiled at the progress he had made. A couple of weeks back, even a week ago, he would never have dared consider something as drastic as that. But he was considering it now. What could Paulson do about it? He examined the question from every angle. Paulson was a powerful and sometimes violent man, but Dackett had noticed him in town yesterday, and the man had seemed stunned. Yes, Ryan's death had knocked a lot out of him. If violence still remained in Paulson, the first expression of it would have a United States marshal on top of him before he knew what happened. These were no longer the days when Dackett had to cautiously feel his way along. He had the help he needed, and he could charge ahead at full tilt. He leaned over the list of evictions he had been making, and at the top of it he penciled the name "Oakes Paulson."

He stepped to the door of his office, opened it, and called, "Find Ross Paulson and tell him I want to see him."

The clerk bobbed his head. "Yes, sir. Right away, sir."

Dackett nodded as he shut the door. That last thought had hit him on the spur of the moment, and he smiled at his cleverness. Oakes Paulson wouldn't do anything to the eviction party he sent out, for Ross Paulson would head it. Oakes wouldn't do anything to his brother, and if that wasn't enough to hold him, Josie Paulson would be. She would stop any violence between them before it started. His smile grew. He wanted to see Oakes's face. The man had caused him considerable trouble and embarrassment. Seeing the gray sickness in his face when he knew he was beaten would be partial repayment. Nothing in the world would stop him from riding out with that eviction party in the morning.

He paced about the room, hitting at his palm with his fist. Ross had better not keep him waiting too long.

It was thirty minutes before Ross came in, and Dackett drew a deep breath to calm himself. "I've got a job for you tomorrow." This man didn't have the stuff of his brother. His manner was subservient, almost fawning. His eyes never could hold quite steady, and they slid away now.

"Anything you say, Mr. Dackett."

He had given Ross a couple of minor jobs before. He suspected Ross would consider steady work, and it amused him to wonder if Ross saw himself in his chair.

"If you work out well on this, maybe I can make it permanent." He caught the raw, leaping eagerness in Ross's face. What he wanted to do was to cuff him to the floor. The man took him for a brainless fool. He acted as though he was sure Dackett knew nothing about him and Reta, when everybody in town had an inkling of what was going on. Now Ross hoped Dackett would support him, too. His next words would erase that eagerness from his face.

"I want you to ride out and serve eviction notice on Oakes Paulson."

He heard the little gasp, something similar to the noise a man made when he was kicked in the stomach. He watched the wildness fill the eyes and enjoyed it. Ross made several false attempts before he could say, "I can't. Anything else—"

"You'll do as I tell you."

My God, this was amazing. There was a spark of courage in the man, for his face seemed to firm, and his eyes held on Dackett's.

"I won't. He's my brother."

Dackett hit his desk a sudden savage blow. "Don't tell me what you will or won't do. Don't you think I know you've been seeing Reta? I'm not blind, nor stupid. You'll ride with that party, or I'll call you out publicly for the other. I'll shoot you down, and people will congratulate me for it." He leaned back in his chair. How savory this cigar suddenly was.

That spark of courage was very short-lived. Ross's face paled, and a nerve ticked in his cheek. "Please." A hand flung out in unconscious supplication. "I'll do anything else. I can't go out there."

"You're going, or I follow you out of this office. When we get to the middle of the street, I'll tell the town what you've been doing." He smiled wolfishly. "You can try to defend yourself. It won't do you a damned bit of good."

That was a noticeable tremble in Ross's hands, and his face was drained of color. He licked his lips before he could speak, and then his voice came out faint and squeaky. "Me going tomorrow morning wouldn't change the—the other."

At least his fright hadn't wiped away his wits. "Reta?" Dackett smiled. "If I had wanted her, wouldn't I have objected before now? You can do as you please after tomorrow."

He saw the shine come into the man's eyes and thought in wonder, Why, he's completely wrapped up in her. He stopped to consider it. Had he ever felt that way about her? If so, it had been very faint and of short duration. He had his brake to apply against Oakes Paulson. Ross's presence out there would manacle him as effectively as a pair of handcuffs.

"You be here in the morning," he warned.

Ross nodded, but his face had a gray sickness.

Dackett sat in his buggy and looked over his force. Quite a cavalcade would ride out to Paulson's. Henshaw and Whelen were there, both mounted, and a United States marshal and two deputies rode in a wagon. Dackett had picked two of the burliest of the railroad workers to make the trip. Ross Paulson was here, too, his face looking even sicker than yesterday, if possible. Dackett thought, He's been drinking, even this early. He had to, even to be able to start the trip.

Nine men were in the party, all armed. Not even the foolhardiest of men would go up against the kind of odds that this group made, not even Oakes Paulson. Despite his assurance, Dackett felt the rigid hollow in his belly deepen as they approached the Paulson house.

He sat his horse in front of the house for a long moment before he made a motion. He had thought the noise of their arrival should have drawn somebody out, but the place was broodingly silent. It would be quite a letdown if nobody was here. But he could still evict Paulson. He could throw his damned furniture into the road and tack the dispossess notice on the front door.

He jerked his head at Ross. "Come on." He stepped out of the buggy and waited impatiently for Ross to join him. Ross's pallid face showed he had no heart in this at all.

Dackett let Ross knock on the door. He looked back at the others, and their faces showed tenseness. Henshaw fidgeted in the saddle, and Dackett cursed him. All of them were scared to death that Oakes Paulson would appear in the doorway.

Josie answered the knock, and she flinched at the sight of her husband. Then her face turned into white marble, with only the eyes showing a bitter hurting. "Why are you here?"

Dackett had never heard more loathing in a voice. He pulled the legal paper from his pocket. "You are evicted, Mrs. Paulson. For nonpayment of a fair and just price."

Her eyes remained on Ross's face. "You were smart enough to pick a time when Oakes isn't around." The contempt in her voice raked him.

"I'm not afraid of Oakes," he growled.

"No?" she jeered. "It's hard to believe the two of you are brothers."

Ross's face flamed. "That's about enough, Josie."

"Why, I haven't even started, Ross. You picked the right kind to run with. You even share the same woman, don't you?"

"I said that's enough!" Ross shouted. He looked at the watching men, and the knowledge that they had heard drove him beyond control. He slapped her, a heavy-handed blow that rapped her head against the wall. She made a sound that was half gasp, half cry of pain, then was silent. Colors took over the cheek, showing the stinging hurt there, but neither hand raised to it. And he hadn't wiped anything away from her eyes.

Ross stared at her a long time, and his face was a frozen emptiness. "Keep your mouth shut, and I won't have to do that again." He turned his head toward Dackett. "All right, Mr. Dackett."

Dackett raised his voice. "Carry this furniture out and pile it in the road. This house doesn't belong to them anymore."

She flinched, and her eyes were sick for a moment, but her head was as high as ever. She stood aside, and men started carrying furniture out to the road. Dackett was near enough to hear her say to Ross, "I think that's why Oakes worried so hard about you. Because he knew you are worthless."

Ross sucked in a tearing breath, and Dackett thought he would hit her again. But his mouth stayed clamped, and he passed her without speaking. He threw the basket of dishes he was carrying at the pile, and the sound of breaking dishes was the beginning of a minor orgy. Perhaps they needed the release of it to break the tension, but nobody was careful anymore with the items they carried from the house. They tossed them at the growing pile instead of setting them down, and Josie's face grew more stricken at each splintering crash.

Dackett watched her with a great deal of interest. She was close to it, but she wasn't going to break. She had enough iron in her to prevent it.

Oakes saw Fessler pounding down the road toward him and pulled up and waited. Fessler's face was agitated, and Oakes thought with gloomy humor, He's getting to be my personal messenger of bad news.

"Oakes, they hit your house," Fessler shouted.

Oakes felt the savage twisting of his heart. "Dackett?"

"Yes. He evicted you. He had your furniture carried out to the road. He smashed up a lot of it."

This rage moved slowly in Oakes, but it consumed thoroughly. "Josie?"

"She's all right. But her face is bruised. She wouldn't tell me how she got it."

Now the rage bounded in Oakes. He had to talk to Josie first before he got on with what had to be done.

"Did she say which way Dackett rode?"

"She thinks toward Baughman's. He had eight men with him." Oakes started to move on, and Fessler cried, "Where are you going?"

Oakes gave him a surprised look. "To see if Josie is all right."

"Then after Dackett?"

Oakes's manner was impatient. "You know that."

"Wait for me at your place, Oakes. You might need help. It won't take me long to round up some of the others." He saw the dissent starting in Oakes's face. "It's our fight, too."

Fessler was right, and Oakes nodded abruptly. "I'll wait."

Fessler went down the road in a mad gallop, and Oakes lifted his reins. Not Josie or Mundro or anybody else would talk him out of a showdown this time.

He found her sitting in one of their chairs, a hopeless, bleak look on her face. She jumped up at the sight of him and ran toward him. He folded her in his arms.

The sobs kept tearing her words apart, and he waited patiently. She cried hard, then said, "Oh damn," and knuckled at her eyes. He pulled out his handkerchief and handed it to her.

She turned a tear-blotched face up to him. "I didn't think I'd go all to pieces like this."

"You had reasons." He congratulated himself that his rage didn't show. But he had seen that bruise on her cheekbone in the first glance. He had waited too long; he had listened too well to caution and wisdom. A man stomped a snake. It took only as simple and as direct an action as that.

He didn't quite touch the spot. "Did Dackett do this?"

She started to shake her head, and he said, "Don't lie to me, Josie."

"It wasn't Dackett." He could barely hear her.

He wanted to shake her for taking so long. "Who, then?"

"Ross."

That stunned him. "He was with them?"

She nodded. "Don't blame him too much, Oakes. I said some awful things to him, things he couldn't stand."

He breathed like a man in great pain. "That's something else I wouldn't look at squarely, Josie. I let it get away from me long ago. Instead of wading in and doing what I knew had to be done with Ross, I kept looking for any little sign of improvement. When will I ever learn that you don't correct anything by running away from it?"

"I shut my eyes, too, Oakes." The tears were coming again.

He patted her awkwardly on the shoulder. He glanced down the road. He wasn't going to wait too long for Fessler.

Chapter Eighteen

Fessler brought a half-dozen men with him. "The word's spreading, more will be coming." His words tumbled out in a breathless rush.

Halderman had a nasty gleam in his eyes. "It's different when it bites you personally, isn't it? You've cost us a lot of time."

Oakes held back angry words. Halderman had a point. Yes, it was different.

"We can carry your furniture back in," Fessler offered. Quick nods ran among the men.

Oakes shook his head. "No, he's got the law on his side. He can dispossess me. But he's going to pay me for the equity I've got here. I put in work and material on this place. He's got to pay me for those things." He was going to collect for something else, too, no matter how many men surrounded Ross. He was going to collect for the abuse to Josie.

He stepped to a bureau and opened a drawer. This piece of furniture belonged in a bedroom, and he felt oddly naked before these watching eyes. He lifted something from the drawer and dropped it into his coat pocket. It made a hard, noticeable bulge.

Josie came to him, and fear made her eyes dark and enormous. "Don't go, Oakes."

He looked at her with steady eyes. "I've got to. It's something I've put off too long as it is." Maybe someday he could go over this in his mind again and picture a different turning, but right now he could see no other course.

Halderman wheeled his horse. "Are we going to get going?" He looked from face to face, savoring his moment. "I could have saved so much time."

Oakes let it pass. His peaceful course only led to the same point as Halderman's violent one had. Only Halderman would have reached the point quicker. He would have paid a bigger price for it, too, Oakes thought wearily. He would have built up a list of dead by now.

They were a half hour behind Dackett's party at Linbled's. Their furniture was in the road, and Mrs. Linbled sat beside it, crying. Linbled was a man in his sixties with a permanent stoop to his shoulders. His face was bewildered, as though this was too big a disaster for him to understand.

He raised dazed eyes to Oakes. "We got put off. They carried our furniture out and said we no longer had any rights to this land. We put in a lot of work here. I don't know what . . ." His voice faded away.

He had put in more than just work, Oakes thought. He had put in caring and hope; he had put in the things that tore a man up harder than just work.

"Did they go on to Gayer's?"

"They headed that way." Linbled's eyes sparked momentarily. "I hope you catch up with them. I'd go with you, but with Mrs. Linbled—" He made a vague gesture that was as inconclusive as his words.

"Sure," Oakes said gently.

They had narrowed the margin to fifteen minutes by the time they reached the Creels. Mrs. Creel was by herself, and Oakes saw more tears. Creel was off somewhere on league business, trying to find where he was needed.

"Catch up with them," Mrs. Creel said passionately. "I hope you kill them all."

Oakes hadn't given that drastic a purpose to this in the beginning, but its possibility grew steadily at the misery he witnessed. They were going to reach one of these houses before Dackett had started carrying out the furniture, or had it all carried out, and then it depended upon how insistent Dackett was about going ahead.

They were five minutes behind at Mollet's, and Mollet was young and a hothead and insisted on going with them. He shook with anger as he told of the guns trained on him while his furniture was carried out. "I'm glad Lisa wasn't here to see this sorry day, Oakes. Wait until I get saddled. I'm going with you."

They lost a few minutes, but nobody objected

too much. Mollett had as big a bill to collect as anybody.

They pounded down the road toward Magee's. Oakes held up his hand and took the speed off the horses when he saw the group of men before Magee's house. There appeared to be an argument going on, but no furniture had been carried out as yet.

Oakes kept the pace to a slow, purposeful walk. Dackett sat in a buggy, and a wagon with five men was drawn up behind it. Dackett hadn't taken any risk of being shorthanded. Oakes's eyes rested on Ross the longest, and he thought he would choke on the waves of his anger.

Halderman looked at Ross with startled eyes, then at Oakes. "My God. Your brother's with him."

The constrained, awkward feeling showed in all their faces, and this development seemed to tie their hands. It wouldn't for long, Oakes thought grimly.

He rode until only a dozen yards separated the two parties.

Dackett slewed around on the buggy seat to watch him, and he couldn't keep the nervousness from his face. "Henshaw," he bellowed. "Get these men off this land. It's railroad property."

Henshaw's roar had a hollow sound. "Take those men away from here, Paulson. You're interfering in lawful business."

Oakes glanced at Bill Whelen. Whelen sat his horse, his face quiet and watchful. Oakes didn't know the United States marshal or his deputy. Oakes would pick Whelen as the most dangerous man of the bunch.

He looked last at Ross. Ross sat with his face half turned away, and Oakes saw the nervous twitch of his lip corners. His hand rested on his thigh, close to the holstered gun, and there was a noticeable tremble in it. Oakes couldn't make Ross meet his eyes. It didn't matter. He would— later.

"You're evicting no more people, Dackett. Until you make arrangements to pay them for the equity they have in their places."

Dackett stared at him open-mouthed. "Are you crazy? Not one of them has paid in a dime."

"No, but they've put in work and materials. The courts will say those things have value. And until these people are paid, you're not moving another one out."

He sat there, big, solid, and indomitable, his eyes drilling into Dackett. Dackett alternately flushed and whitened. Then he turned toward Ross. "Ross, get in that house and start moving out that furniture."

Ross paled, and his eyes pleaded with Dackett.

"Move, damn it, I won't tell you again."

It was a clever move on Dackett's part, Oakes thought. Dackett had changed the focus of this thing, and everybody was thrown off-balance. He felt the sour sickness roll in his belly. Dackett had some kind of a hard clamp on Ross.

Ross's weakness was there for all to see, and shame consumed Oakes. "Ross, ride over here where you belong." The anger didn't distort his voice too much.

He couldn't believe it. Ross wasn't moving. He just sat there, his eyes still begging Dackett.

Oakes swung down. "I'm going to beat hell out of you, Ross. You've earned it for what you did to Josie."

Ross's face turned wild. "Stay where you are, Oakes."

Oakes kept up that slow plodding. Ross threw a final pleading look at Dackett. Dackett wouldn't release him either. A sob broke in his throat. He was caught between the two of them.

His face shattered, and he clawed at his pistol. "Stay back, Oakes. I mean it."

Oakes hesitated the briefest of pauses at the sight of the drawn gun. "Put it away, Ross."

But Ross had been pushed too far by two relentless men, and between them, they had broken him. He screamed an incoherent phrase and fired at Oakes.

Oakes felt a nasty plucking at his coat sleeve. Dackett's face had a malignant shine as he slapped at his gun. He was grabbing his chance to get into this. Oakes clawed at his coat pocket, trying to get his gun free. His hand was around the butt, but some other part of the weapon was caught in his pocket. He made a frantic jerk, and the pocket tore free of the coat. He raised and fired hastily, positive Dackett would get off a shot before he did.

Dackett was standing in the buggy, and Oakes's shot took him in the throat. The strangest wondering look crossed Dackett's face. He wanted desperately to say something, but he couldn't force words through the quick spring fountain of blood. He broke at the waist, striking a wheel as he fell to the ground.

Oakes threw himself down. A bullet kicked sand in front of his face, and he rolled hastily. The firing was general from both sides, and a shotgun boomed from the wagon. He heard a man's scream rise higher and higher, then break off in mid-note. As the volume of firing intensified, he thought, My God, no one will come out of this alive.

He looked frantically about for Ross, and Ross was running, kicking furiously against his horse's flanks in a demand for greater speed.

The screaming and firing seemed to grow in savage, wild volume, and Oakes saw Mollet clutch at his chest before he sagged from his saddle.

Stinging particles filled his eyes, and for a moment he couldn't see. He heard the thud of hooves, and by the time his eyes had cleared, Henshaw was charging him. He leaned far over, firing as he came, but the gun made no impression on Oakes. It was those slashing hooves, looming larger and larger, that filled him with fear, and he rolled in desperate haste. It seemed inevitable that a hoof had to strike him, and he waited for the numbing shock. The horse was past him before Oakes realized that he hadn't been hit.

Henshaw wheeled his horse around to make another run at him, and Oakes came up on one knee. He aimed with slow deliberation, and the shot picked Henshaw out of the saddle.

Men were down all over the place. Fessler was on his hands and knees, his bloody head hanging low. Baughman was trying to pull himself along the ground and making crippled, broken progress of it. Two men were draped over the sides of the wagon, and another was running for his life across the yard. Whelen was firing a shotgun into the air while yelling at the top of his voice, and Oakes thought wonderingly, He's trying to stop it. He swung his pistol off Whelen, looking for another target, and saw none that stood out with clarity. All the belligerent, driving purpose that had made them stand out so clearly before was gone, and he saw only broken, wounded, or dead men.

He stood, and it took amazing effort. How long had it lasted? A few seconds at the most. Ross's fear-crazed shot had plunged them all into a hell that would never be forgotten.

Movement caught the corner of his eye, and he turned his head. Halderman was mounted and driving in the direction Ross had taken. What had happened here wasn't enough for Halderman; he had to have Ross.

It took valuable time to catch up a horse, to put it into full speed. For a frightening moment he thought he had lost Halderman; then he saw horse and man bobbing up ahead between the trees.

He gained on him, but it seemed so slow. He could only hope that Ross had enough lead so that Halderman could never catch him.

Oakes had halved the gap between himself and Halderman by the time they crested the hill. The descent broke sharply on the other side, and halfway down the slope, Oakes saw the form of a horse struggling to rise. The picture was clear. Ross had taken this slope too fast, and his horse had fallen. Its helpless attempts to rise showed that it had broken a foreleg.

At the bottom of the hill a running figure looked back over its shoulder, then tried to find additional speed that its legs didn't have.

Halderman saw Ross, too, for his long, keening yell carried back to Oakes. He wasn't going to be in time to stop Halderman from doing whatever he had in mind.

Ross threw another frightened look over his shoulder. He saw how the horse was cutting down his advantage, and he suddenly stopped and turned.

Oakes thought for an instant that resistance might be in his mind, but it wasn't. Ross's hands went into the air, and he held them there.

Halderman slowed his horse. His pistol was out, and Oakes thought at first that Halderman intended taking Ross in. Then Halderman stopped his horse a dozen feet from Ross. If he was saying something to Ross, Oakes was too far away to hear it.

Oakes's blood chilled as Halderman raised his pistol. He yelled and drove his horse harder, and the report of a pistol carried too plainly to him. For a moment he thought nothing had happened, that he had imagined the shot, for Ross still stood. But the expression on his face had changed; it had now a curiously childish look of hurt. His mouth opened, but Oakes never knew whether or not he said anything. He tried to keep his balance, then he plunged forward on his face.

For an agonized moment, thought and action were frozen in Oakes. Ross was on the ground, and Halderman was on his horse, looking at him. It was all before Oakes, and it still couldn't have happened.

He threw off the paralyzing bonds that held him. It was a long shot for a pistol, made more difficult by shooting from a running horse, but Oakes went for it. He yelled savage obscenities at Halderman, and as the startled man jerked his horse around, he fired. Halderman's horse reared, and Oakes didn't know whether it was caused by the closeness of his bullet or the alarm his rush made. But when the animal came down, Halderman was still in the saddle, fighting to aim his gun at Oakes.

Oakes fired again, and Halderman swayed. He seemed to be making some awful effort to keep his gun hand raised, but it sagged on him. The gun fell first, and Halderman clung to the horn with his left hand, while his horse broke into a full run. Slowly, Halderman leaned more and more to one side, until he overbalanced and fell to the ground.

He bounced as he hit, and he wasn't sitting up by the time Oakes reached him. The spreading stain grew on his shoulder, and his face showed both the shock of the fall and of the wound.

Oakes threw off and ran a few steps before he killed his momentum. Halderman quailed before Oakes's eyes. He tried a couple of times before he could get the words out. "Oakes, he was one of them."

"You bastard." It was said without fervor and the more terrifying for it. Oakes looked as though he were seeing some strange new specimen for the first time. He slowly raised his pistol.

"No, Oakes." Halderman's voice rose until its notes were shrill and piercing. "I had to do it. He fired the first shot. He got good men killed."

"You could have arrested him," Oakes said almost absently.

Halderman had trouble talking. Spittle formed bubbles at his lips, broke, and ran down his chin, and he was unaware of it. "You can't do it, Oakes. I only did what I had to."

"Then I'll only do what I have to." The pistol was leveled at Halderman's face. It wasn't going to be hard to do at all.

He heard his name shouted, and he had the feeling it had been called before, but this was the first time he had really heard it. He turned his head, and Bill Whelen rode as hard as he could toward him.

"Don't do it, Oakes," Whelen yelled. "Goddamn it, haven't enough men died today?"

It had no sense of reality; it had no power to touch Oakes at all. He let Whelen drive on toward him and dismount. Whelen showed no gun, and even if he had one leveled on Oakes he couldn't stop him.

"Eight men are dead or dying, Oakes. Isn't that enough of a score for you?"

"I'm going to kill him, Bill. He shot Ross down without giving him a chance. Ross was trying to surrender."

Whelen nodded gravely. "I saw it all, Oakes.

But if you kill him, I'm arresting you for murder. It'll stick. And I'll see you hanged for it."

Oakes looked bewildered. "But he killed Ross, he—" He stopped and fumbled for words, and nothing came to his mind.

"I told you I saw it. If you'll get out of my way, I'll take him in for murder. And what I promised you goes for him."

He saw the haggardness grow in Oakes's face and the shaking come into his hands. "Don't you want Josie to have anything left out of this?"

Oakes hadn't thought of her until Whelen said her name. Suddenly, the full import of the senseless violence rolled in on him, and he thought he would vomit.

Whelen wasn't quite sure of him yet. "Oakes, I promise I'll tell this exactly the way it happened. The railroad side started it."

Oakes opened his hand and let the pistol fall. He thought his knees would buckle and dump him. "Take him in, Bill." His voice was a brittle rustle of sound. "I'll bring in Ross."

Chapter Nineteen

The deputy United States marshal rebuffed Mundro for the third time that day. "Nobody sees the prisoners." He made an unconscious appeal for sympathy. "I'm only following my orders."

Mundro raised his voice. He wanted the small crowd behind him to hear what he had to say. "What are you so afraid of, Deputy, that you have to hide it? And tell us where your orders come from."

The deputy flushed. "My orders come through the court. You know that."

"Ah, but tell us who gives the courts the orders. That's the one we want to hear you name. Are you afraid to name the railroad, Deputy?"

The deputy's face turned brick-red. "Go on, or I'll arrest you."

Mundro faced the crowd. "Did you hear that? I'm to be arrested for telling the truth. Did you know it's now a federal offense?"

"I can arrest you for inciting a riot."

Mundro leaned toward him, his face aflame. "Maybe it's time for the people to riot, Deputy. When their law is ordered by one company. When that company can hold prisoners without anybody being able to talk to them, when that company can stop all communications going out or coming into an entire valley, I'd say it was time for the people to do something. You know that not a word can move by telegraph. They're afraid of that truth, too, wouldn't you say?"

Mundro had a good range of voice. He pulled people from a half block away, and they hurried to join the crowd.

The deputy's eyes grew more harried. He glanced behind him at the jail door as though hoping to see help. "All I know is that those people in there were arrested for blocking a United States marshal in the performance of his duty. He was killed in that performance."

"Ah, but who opened fire first? Tell us that, Deputy. That's what we're waiting to hear."

The deputy's face was getting wild. "How do I know? I wasn't out there."

"You should've been. Then you'd know you've put the wrong people in jail. Does the railroad think that keeping the news bottled up will keep the outside world from knowing the truth?"

Galen was worried on that score, for he didn't know the truth himself. But it had to be unfavorable to the railroad, or they wouldn't be hiding it like this. Nobody had been able to talk to the prisoners since their arrest.

The deputy made a futile show of rage. "I'm warning you not to hang around here. I won't be warning you again." He stomped into the jail and slammed the door behind him.

Mundro watched him with a contemplative smile. There went a worried man.

He tried to make his way through the crowd, and hands reached out from every side to stop him. How could he answer any of their questions when he didn't know for sure himself what had happened? All he knew for certain was that five men were dead, and the doctors said the other three were dying. How could Fessler live with his right side torn away, and Baughman had twelve heavy buckshot that went clear through his chest. It was a miracle that either of them had lived this long. A rifle and a shotgun were aggressive weapons. Four on the railroad side were dead, all of them killed by pistol fire. Wouldn't the doctors agree that a pistol was only a weapon of self-defense?

Both doctors had bristled under Mundro's badgering. They weren't building any case for him. They hadn't been out there; they didn't know what had happened.

Mundro raised his voice above the clamor of the questions. "I'll tell you this. The truth can't be hidden. I've got a rider on the way now with the story. If he can't find a telegraph station that's open, he'll ride clear to San Francisco."

They cheered him for a long moment before they let him go. The only trouble was that he didn't have all the truth as yet. He had written only a skeleton framework, not fleshed with the details. And so much could depend upon the details. He needed to know what kind of intentions were in the settlers' minds when they caught up with Dackett's party, for there was no doubt they had pursued them. One of the missing details loomed more important with every passing minute, for it could shift the picture all around. Who fired the first shot? The answer to that would point out aggressor and defender; it would carry tremendous weight, both moral and legal.

He heard his name called and turned his head. His heart sank. He wished Josie wasn't here, but he knew nothing could have kept her away.

He crossed the street and took her hands, noticing how white and strained her face was. If she hadn't heard about Ross, it would leave the awful duty of breaking it on him. She looked dry-eyed enough, but a woman could expend the bulk of her tears in a relatively brief time.

He swallowed hard. "Josie, do you know about Ross?"

She nodded, and it didn't seem to tear her apart.

"I'm sorry." It was a banal thing to say, but he could think of nothing else.

"It's Oakes I want to hear about."

He looked at her more keenly. She didn't flinch under his inspection. Ah, he thought, I wonder if Oakes knows.

"None of us have seen him, Josie. But we hear he isn't hurt."

She closed her eyes briefly. She didn't intend to confirm his suspicions, but she couldn't help it.

"Josie, did Ross come home before Oakes rode after Dackett?"

It was her turn to show surprise. "Ross wasn't with Oakes. He was with Dackett." She related the scene, and though she dwelt only lightly on Ross's blow, Mundro guessed what had set Oakes off. It had been brother against brother and the more ugly for it. He couldn't help but wonder who had fired the bullet that killed Ross. He hoped that burden wasn't on Oakes.

He took her arm. "Are you going back home tonight?"

"Home?" Her face was bitter. "All our furniture is sitting in the road. A great deal of it is broken."

"Dackett ordered it?"

"Yes. I don't want to go back out there again, Galen."

He nodded in sympathy. He had another fact. A few of the murky shadows were dissipating, letting the picture come clearer. No authority in the land could blame a man for defending home and person.

He smiled at her. "First we get you something to eat, then see about a room for the night."

His smile didn't banish all of her fears. "Will Oakes be all right, Galen?"

He gave it serious consideration. "I think so. You've told me things that can do nothing else but help him. No wonder the railroad shut off all telegraph wires." He smiled again at her questioning look. He would explain that to her later.

He questioned her during supper about who had been in Dackett's party. She knew Henshaw and Whelen. She had noticed the man with the marshal's badge, but she didn't know his name. She knew two of the railroad workers in the wagon; the others were unknown to her.

Mundro's eyes narrowed in thought. He had seen Whelen not over an hour ago. The man had been Henshaw's deputy, and that could make an impenetrable wall. But suppose he might talk, suppose he might tell just what had happened out there?

He took Josie to the hotel. "Will you be all right for tonight? Can I get you anything else?"

She shook her head with weary indifference. "I wish I could talk to Oakes."

He pressed her hand. "I wish both of us could."

He found Whelen in the last saloon he looked in. Whelen sat at a table by himself, and he was half drunk. It didn't show in his face or movements, but it was a feeling that flowed strongly from him.

His eyes burned as Mundro sat down. "Don't you know I'm a leper? The rest of them know it. Look how they avoid me."

He poured himself a drink with a steady hand.

He lifted it in a mocking gesture, then tossed it down.

Mundro signaled the bartender for a drink. "That's because you were on the wrong side."

A degree of sullenness crept into Whelen's face. "What else could I do? I was paid to do a job, any job that Henshaw pointed out. And he did what Dackett told him."

"But you fought for Dackett." A tingle of excitement stirred in Mundro. He always felt it when something favorable was about to break.

"I stayed out of it," Whelen shouted. "I fired into the air and tried to break it up. But after it got started, no one listened to anything." He frowned in a puzzled way. "It was over quicker than a man could sneeze. Men were down all over. Why I wasn't hit—" He let a shaking head finish it for him.

"Bill, who started it?"

Whelen stared at him, and Mundro thought miserably, He's not going to say any more. The railroad's got their hold on him. "Do you want to live in this town?"

Whelen glared at him. "It's my home."

"But you don't want to live here like a leper, do you? Then tell the people you were there without any part in it." A thought struck him, and his eyes gleamed. "They're going to need a new sheriff. Why slam that door in your face when you can have the job?"

He heard Whelen's quickened breathing as the idea seized him. "Do you think so?"

Mundro grinned. "No guarantee, but it's possible. I can promise they'll know just the part you played. What happened out there?"

"Ross Paulson started it."

Mundro didn't know whether to be elated or depressed. It depended on which side Ross was on when the fight started. Josie said the railroad's. If Whelen would only confirm it—

"Where was Ross?"

Whelen squinted, trying to recall. "Right beside Dackett's buggy. I think."

"He rode out there with Dackett?"

Whelen nodded, and Mundro could let his elation swell. "Were the settlers looking for a fight?"

Whelen frowned. "I don't think they knew what they were looking for. Oakes said Dackett had to stop throwing people off until he did something about the work and materials they had in their land. Dackett ordered Ross to go ahead and start carrying out furniture. Oakes said something about him whipping him. He climbed down and started toward Ross, and Ross went crazy. He fired at Oakes and blew everything wide open."

Mundro breathed out a soft "Ah." The railroad had started that fight. "Go on."

Whelen made a helpless gesture. "It's kinda blurred. It all happened so fast. Dackett shot at Oakes, missed him, and Oakes killed him. Ross ran right after he fired. Halderman took after him, and Oakes went after both of them. I followed in time to see Halderman kill Ross. I was sure I couldn't stop Oakes from killing Halderman. He'd already wounded him. I would have had to arrest him for murder."

Mundro let out a long sigh. If Whelen would repeat this story, it was proof that the railroad was the instigator. At least that much onus was taken from the settlers' shoulders.

But how would he use it? He discarded one approach after another. His face brightened. Judge Mackail. He was a local judge, with authority limited accordingly. He was an old man but still peppery, and a stickler for justice regardless of who was involved. Mundro felt sure his authority extended far enough to permit somebody to talk to the prisoners. He grinned wolfishly. That alone could cause the railroad to do some scrambling to abandon the position it had taken.

"Bill, will you tell the same thing to Judge Mackail?"

Whelen shook his head, then grinned at the dismay flooding Mundro's face. "Not tonight. And maybe not tomorrow. I saw him before I rode out with Dackett this morning. He was on his way to Fresno for something. But he's an old man, and he doesn't like to be away from home for long."

Mundro sighed. More waiting. It was going to be hard on him and harder on Josie. The railroad would use the time to pour out more inflammatory words against the settlers. As it was, too many people were already condemning them.

Chapter Twenty

Mundro looked at Oakes anxiously, as the deputy marshal unlocked the cell door.

"I guess I'll be doing nothing else but unlocking this damned door," the man growled.

Mundro grinned coldly. "That's what the judge ordered you to do, isn't it? Give the prisoners their right to see certain people?"

The vinegary little judge had been outraged at the railroad's handling of this affair. He had returned from Fresno last night, and Mundro had his writ, restoring certain rights to Oakes this morning. Those two days of being held incommunicado were going to hurt the railroad far more than they had Oakes and the others.

"Oakes, are they treating you all right?"

Oakes grinned. "The food could be better." His face sobered quickly. "Josie?"

"She's fine. You'll see her before long. Whelen told me what happened. Judge Mackail pried the railroad's hands off you."

Oakes's face had a black and brooding look. "It was a bad morning, Galen. I don't think anybody had any idea of it going like that or that far. I'm glad the judge sees it a little our way."

"That won't do you any good, Oakes. The railroad won't let the case be tried here. Too much public sympathy on your side around here. The railroad knows this is going to blacken them. They'll move the trial to San Francisco, where they can come closer to controlling things. They've got to get a conviction against you to make themselves appear a little better."

He shook his head at the dismay flooding Oakes's face. "Figure they'll get their conviction, Oakes. But I'll bet it will only be a token one. Even their courts and judges won't dare go beyond that. It's going to take a long time to break their power completely, Oakes, but you've beaten them. The public sees them for what they are, and that's the biggest victory. The other things will follow."

Mundro might consider that they had won, but Oakes didn't. He would never be able to buy land in this valley, regardless of how high he was willing to pay for it. The railroad would block every attempt he made to settle here.

"I hope I don't win any more fights this way."

Mundro laughed. "This won't hurt you any. California's got lots of land. Other communities will want you after this fight. And they'll make it as easy for you as they can. You've lost mostly time. That's all it's cost you."

Oakes couldn't brighten too much. It had taken money to live, and he had bought materials to put into that place. No, it had also cost money, but he and Josie still had the bulk of the money from Ohio left. A disturbing thought struck him.

Half of that money was hers. What would be left wouldn't buy him a great deal of land.

"It's going to turn out bad," he said wearily. "I started losing the day I left Ohio."

He was glad when Mundro left. He appreciated Mundro's trying to buoy him up, but Mundro saw all this from too bright an angle. The man who wasn't in a fix always had more optimism than the man who was.

He stretched out on the hard bunk and stared at the ceiling. He wondered what Josie would do. Probably go back to her family in Ohio, he thought heavily. There was nothing here to hold her longer. He heard light footsteps coming down the corridor, and despite his melancholy mood his heart leaped.

He turned his head toward the cell door, and Reta was there. She gripped the bars with an intensity that whitened her knuckles, and her eyes were naked and vulnerable. He stood and hardened his face. He had nothing he wanted to say to her and nothing he wanted to hear.

"Oakes." The name barely carried to him. "I thought I would die until I learned you were all right."

He had a savage desire to hurt her, and he swung a brutal club. "Your husband isn't."

Passion distorted her face, and she smoothed it with effort.

He watched her with an odd curiosity. He

wondered if any of her actions ever caused her real sorrow. He threw another blow at her. "And Ross isn't."

She shut her eyes briefly. "And you blame me for that."

In all fairness, he couldn't blame her for the weakness that had been in Ross, but he could blame her for seizing upon it and directing it the way it had gone.

"Oakes, don't you see it was the only way I could keep my contact with you? Do you want me to beg? I will."

She managed to squeeze tears from her eyes as she stretched a hand through the bars toward him. He felt a little sickened. None of what had happened meant anything to her except that it had opened up a new approach. "Go away, Reta." He started to turn away.

"Oakes, wait. Have you no pity? I've never had a strong man to love me. And I need one. Quincy, Ross—" Her gesture dismissed them. "Oakes, I can help you. I'm a wealthy woman now. I'll put all of it into the fight to save you. I'll—"

He threw back his head and laughed, and his laughter wasn't forced. "Why, Reta, being owned by you would put me in a worse fix than I am now."

She stared in slack-mouthed disbelief. It took her a long time to realize that the laugh was real, that he meant it.

Her face turned alternately white and pink, and she breathed in tearing sobs. She had stripped herself naked before him, and it meant nothing.

Her laughter was too shrill. "Did you believe me? What would I do with a great, stupid oaf like you? What would I do—" She couldn't stop the tears from springing into her eyes, and she ducked her head.

He thought in astonishment, If she isn't actually in love with me, she thinks she is. And at the moment it amounted to the same thing.

He made his voice as gentle as possible. "Reta, I'm sorry," and oddly enough he meant it.

She raised her head, and her eyes blazed at him through her tears. "I hope they hang you."

He chuckled wryly. "And I hope you don't get your hope."

She put a hating look on him, but she couldn't hold it. She was running as she went down the corridor. The deputy waited for her at the end of the hall. He gave Oakes an odd look before he shut the door behind her.

Oakes lay down on the bunk again. He locked his hands behind his head and stared at the ceiling. He wouldn't want to go through any more episodes like that. He heard the light sound of footsteps again and groaned. She was back with some new argument he would have to beat down.

"Is everybody in town going to visit you?" the deputy growled. Then a much softer voice said, "Oakes."

It jerked him upright in a hurry, and it was odd, but he couldn't speak. All he could do was to stare, and he had never thought the sight of her could hurt so much.

"Josie!" He didn't even recognize the sound of his own voice. He bounded to his feet and ran to the bars. He grabbed for both of her hands, and she seemed as eager for him to take them.

"Oakes," she whispered. "You're all right?"

"I'm fine now." He couldn't understand why she clung to him so. She had been through a bad time, and maybe that was the cause of all this feeling.

"What's going to happen, Oakes?"

His face sobered. "I don't know. Galen thinks we'll be tried someplace else. He thinks we'll get a light sentence. But nobody's sure of anything, Josie."

She stared at him in quick anguish. "But it isn't fair."

He held her hands harder. Fair! That was a goal men strived so hard to reach. And they didn't make it very many times.

Her face twisted with some painful memory. "Oakes, I couldn't cry about Ross. I tried. I couldn't."

It had happened to him. He had known pain

without the relief of tears. What was she trying to tell him? That the Ross who had died was not the Ross she had known and loved?

"It was over between us, Oakes. I tried to make it work. I tried—" She was crying now, a soft flutter of sound.

He tried to console her, and swore at himself for his awkwardness. "I know, Josie," he said over and over.

"You don't know." Her eyes sparkled with tears. "Everything you did made him look so small and mean. I tried not to compare you. I couldn't help it. Oh, Oakes—" The hard crying drowned her words.

Knowledge dawned in his eyes. Even in his dreams he had never let himself reach this point. Surely he was dreaming now.

She raised her face to him. "Oakes, can't you help me?"

He started to grab for her through the bars. Then the realization of too many things hit him. What did he have to offer her? He faced a prison sentence. Mundro thought it would be light, but that was a long way from making it so. Who was going to look after her during all that time? There was only one practical course left, and he knew he had to take it.

"Josie!" He made no attempt to blunt the sharpness in his voice. "You're going back home to your folks."

Dismay flooded her face. "You don't want me to stay?"

He couldn't look at her. "No. I want you to leave today." The arrangements about the money were secondary. She could have it all if she needed it.

"Oakes, look at me."

He tried to steel his face, and it broke miserably, giving him away.

"Why are you lying to me?"

"Damn it, Josie. Because I don't know what's ahead. I could be sent to prison for a long time."

"But you don't want me to go?"

He could lie to her again, but he had completely betrayed himself. "No, but I'm not going to let you stay."

Her voice held laughter and tears. "I don't see how you can help yourself very much." Her fingers walked up his arms, and her hands seized him, trying to pull him closer to her.

He bent his head nearer to her face. "Josie." Damned if the tears weren't springing into his eyes.

"Oh, Oakes."

Her lips were very near his mouth. He quit trying to deny the most obvious fact in the world. It would be impossible for him to send her away—regardless of what was ahead.

Epilogue

Mundro had been right on every count. The trial was held in San Francisco, and the verdict rendered a few days before Christmas. A multitude of words about it had been published in the San Francisco papers, and public opinion lashed at the Southern Pacific in angry waves. The only charge against the defendants that had a chance of sticking was that of resisting a United States officer in the performance of his duty. The railroad had badly wanted a conspiracy charge against the settlers. It would have washed their hands for them very nicely. But the more the volume of testimony mounted, the more it blackened the railroad. Oakes would never forget the way Josie looked the day the jury brought in the verdict. Her head was held high, her face was composed, but she couldn't still the trembling of her lips. He had thought her knees would collapse when the jury reported it had found the settlers guilty of resisting the officer, innocent on all other charges. The sentence was eight months to be served in the San Jose jail.

There was only one bad thing about the San Jose jail: its monotony. The treatment and food were good, it was only the confinement that galled a man. And that wasn't too strict.

Oakes took another turn about the room. His quarters were on the second floor of the jail, and he wouldn't be getting out of them today, for it wasn't his turn to get the mail. He smiled at the memory of the first few days here. Everybody had treated them as though they were welcome guests instead of prisoners. Telegrams of sympathy had flooded the jail, and a few cables had even arrived from Europe. William Curtis, the jailer, had soon tired of running up the steps with each fresh batch of messages. He gave the settlers a fishline and hooked the wires to it; the wires were then pulled up through the window.

But even that proved too much of a chore for Curtis. "If so many people think so much of you, I guess it proves you won't run away. Here's the key to the jail. Get your own mail."

From then on, one of them had gone after it every day. Oakes hadn't wanted for visitors and amusements. Fred Black's grocery store had sent them groceries free of charge, and the St. James Hotel provided breakfasts each morning for the four without cost. Mundro got down every few weeks, and he was still delighting in annoying the railroad with every barb he could find. Best of all, Josie came every day. No, he couldn't say this incarceration had been rough in any degree, but still a restlessness drove him, and he knew its source. Half of his sentence had been served; it was well into spring; and his hands itched to work the earth again. Whenever he looked at Josie, she became part of his ache. She and the land were tied together in his wanting. He scowled at the walls. She hadn't been here yesterday, and she hadn't been here so far today.

He moved to the door to yell at Curtis to ask him if he had heard or seen any sign of her, and Mundro was coming down the hall.

Oakes's frown faded. He had a fondness for this stubborn little man. Between them they had attacked a huge abuse. They hadn't thoroughly whipped it, but they had forced it to retreat.

Mundro came into the cell, and Oakes put a sour look on him. "Why are you so happy?" He was a little surprised to see him today. It had only been last week that he was here.

"I just learned the railroad has reduced the land value set by their grader by twelve and a half percent. I doubt if we can pry any more out of them."

"It's still far above the price they put out in their circulars."

"It is. But we did make them back up a step, Oakes. The new adjusted price will still be too high for a lot of the settlers. They'll lose their land. But we did win a victory of sorts. The railroad will be a little more cautious in future dealings with the public."

"And you're satisfied with that?"

Mundro shrugged. "Yes. We could have gotten

nothing." He pulled a letter from his pocket. "Here's an offer you might be interested in. It's on a piece of land up around Merced. A widow wants to sell it. I looked at it. I think you'll like it. You won't have any trouble getting financial help if you need it."

The restlessness vanished. He could have his land. Though he couldn't be on it for a while, he would own it, and that was almost as good.

"Galen, tie it up for me. Don't take any chance of losing it."

Mundro grinned. "I thought you'd feel that way. I already have."

The gloom of the day was all gone. Now all he needed was to tell Josie about this. "Galen, Josie hasn't been in for the last two days. Find her for me. See if something's wrong."

Mundro had a thoughtful look. "Something's bothering her. She wouldn't talk to me at all."

Oakes felt a stab of fear. Could it be possible that she was sorry for her bargain, that she couldn't face the restrictions of four more months of this kind of life? Not Josie, he denied. But a man could never be positive.

He gripped Mundro's shoulder. "Find her. I've got to talk to her."

"I won't have far to look. Here she comes now."

Oakes thought her face looked subdued as she came inside. He seized her hands. "Josie, have you been sick?"

She shook her head. She kept her gaze on the floor, and he couldn't make her look at him.

"Not sick, Oakes. Weary of this kind of living."

His heart plummeted. He had guessed right. "But Josie, it'll be over in such a short time. Four months—"

"It isn't a short time. And I'm tired of waiting."

He was frantic, and the words stuck in his throat. He looked to Mundro for help, and Mundro stared at the ceiling.

Josie stepped to the door and called, "Mr. Curtis, is it ready?"

"Ready," Curtis replied.

Mundro took his arm. "Come on, Oakes."

Oakes tried to jerk free. He didn't want to go with Mundro; he had to stay and talk to her.

"You'd better go with him," she said in a flat voice.

He looked back over his shoulder as Mundro led him down the hall. Josie followed with her gaze on the floor. He didn't want any more surprises this morning. He would never recover from the one he'd already had.

Curtis opened the door to two rooms at the end of the hall, and he beamed all over his face. Oakes barely glanced at them. They looked as though they had been newly furnished, and maybe a woman's touch was in the curtains at the windows. But what did he give a damn about that? He wanted to talk to Josie.

She came up to him, and now she looked at him. Her eyes danced, and a tremulous smile was on her lips. "I am tired of living this kind of life, Oakes. And I will not wait four more months. Mr. Curtis suggested we honeymoon here, and he helped me with the rooms. He had to do the work, for I couldn't let you see me. Oh, Oakes. Don't raise any foolish objections."

A hundred objections rushed to his tongue. A man didn't get married in a jail, and he didn't spend his honeymoon in one. He looked at the wide smiles on Mundro's and Curtis's faces; he looked at the love in her face, and not an objection survived.

He opened his arms wide to her. "Objections, Josie? What are those?"

Center Point Large Print
600 Brooks Road / PO Box 1
Thorndike, ME 04986-0001 USA

(207) 568-3717

US & Canada:
1 800 929-9108
www.centerpointlargeprint.com